THE Officially Awesome SCOOBY-DOO! ACTIVITY BOOK

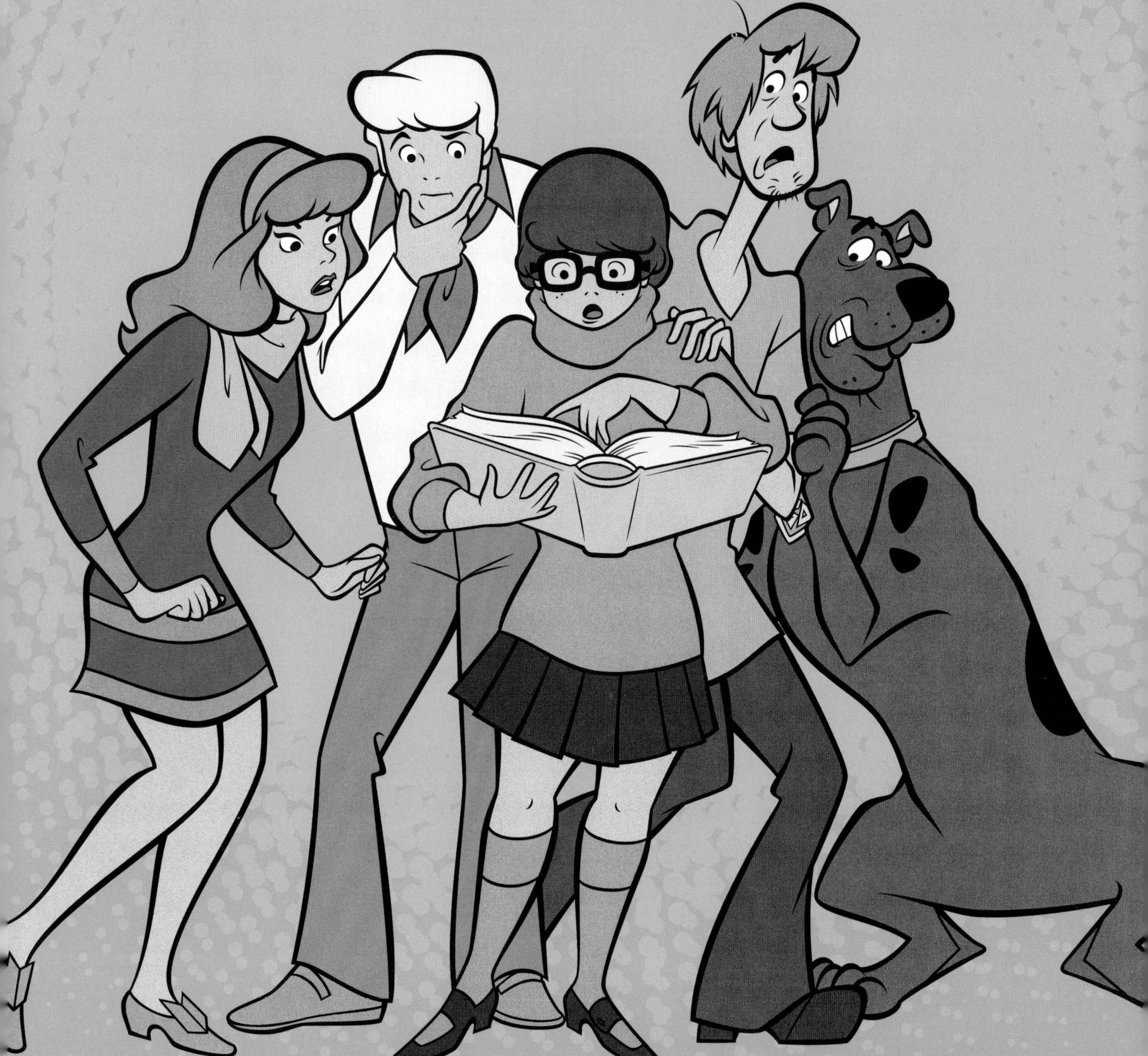

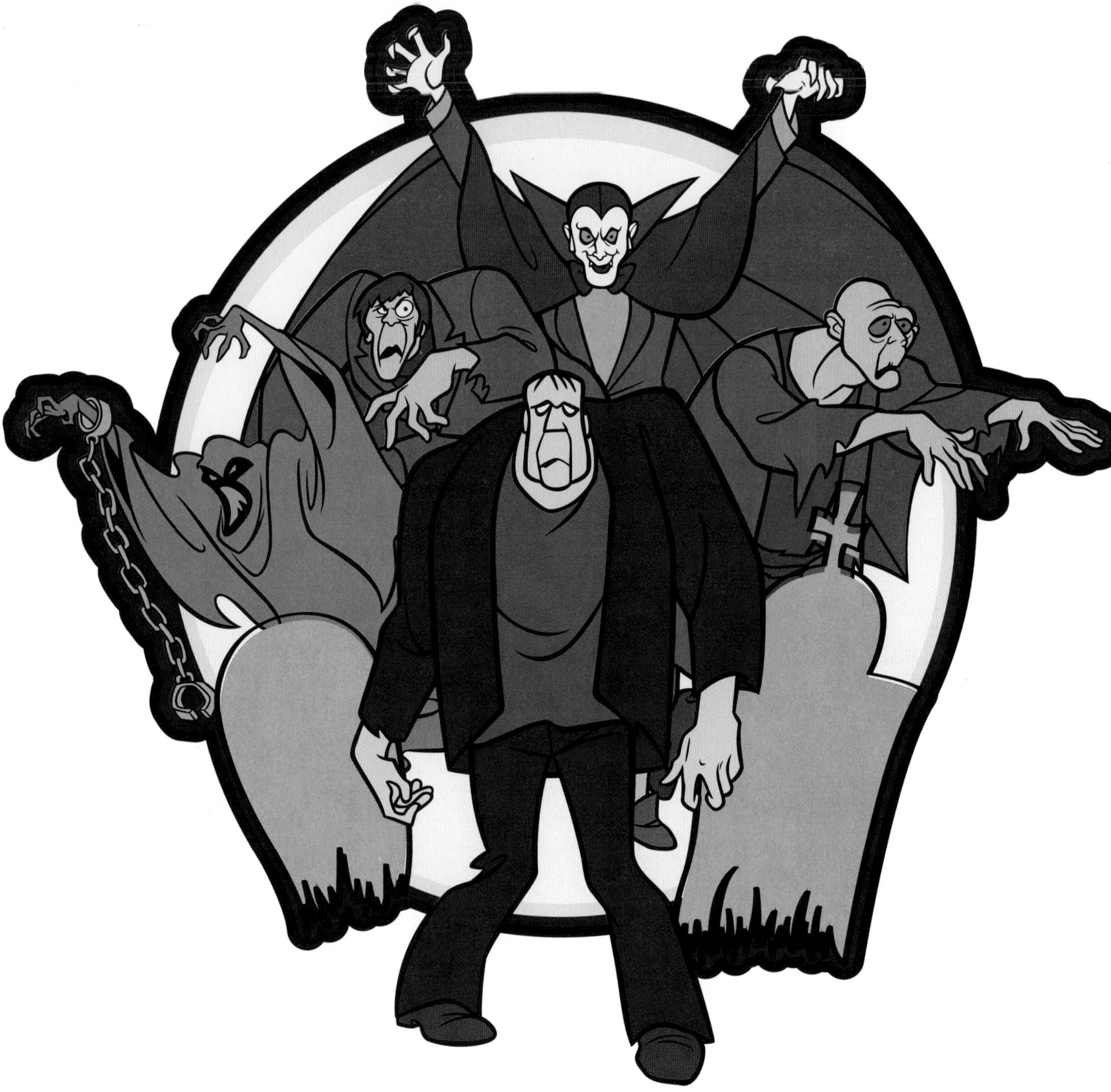

Produced by

DOWNTOWN BOOKWORKS INC.

President Julie Merberg
Editorial Director Sarah Parvis
Managing Editor LeeAnn Pemberton
Editorial Assistant Katarina Lazo

Redesigned by Brian Michael Thomas/Our Hero Productions

Special Thanks Patty Brown, Kathy Gordon, Janice Wilcoxson

Publisher Richard Fraiman
General Manager Steven Sandonato
Executive Director, Marketing Services Carol Pittard
Executive Director, Retail & Special Sales Tom Mifsud
Executive Director, New Product Development Peter Harper
Director, Bookazine Development & Marketing Laura Adam
Publishing Director Joy Butts
Assistant General Counsel Helen Wan
Book Production Manager Susan Chodakiewicz
Design & Prepress Manager Anne-Michelle Gallero
Associate Brand Manager Melissa Joy Kong
Associate Prepress Manager Alex Voznesenskiy
Special thanks Victoria Alfonso, Christine Austin, Jeremy Biloon, Glenn Buonocore, Malati Chavali, Jim Childs, Rose Cirrincione, Jacqueline Fitzgerald, Christine Font, Lauren Hall, Carrie Hertan, Suzanne Janso, Malena Jones, Mona Li, Robert Marasco, Kimberly Marshall, Amy Migliaccio, Dave Rozzelle, Ilene Schreider, Adriana Tierno, Jonathan White, Vanessa Wu

ISBN 10: 1-60320-187-4
ISBN 13: 978-1-60320-187-2

Published by Time Home Entertainment Inc.
135 West 50th Street New York, New York 10020

We welcome your comments and suggestions about Time Home Entertainment Books. Please write to us at: Time Home Entertainment Inc., Attention: Book Editors, PO Box 11016, Des Moines, IA 50336-1016. If you would like to order any of our hardcover Collector's Edition books, please call us at 1-800-327-6388. (Monday through Friday, 7:00 a.m.–8:00 p.m. or Saturday, 7:00 a.m.–6:00 p.m. Central Time.)

1 QGD 11

Table of Contents

MYSTERY INC. NEEDS YOU!

Become an official Mystery Inc. detective by making your very own badge!

What to do:

1. Cut out the front and the back of the badge.

2. Glue the two pieces back to back.

3. Stick on a photo of yourself and fill in your top-secret details!

Meet the Gang

We've dug into the Mystery Inc. filing cabinet to get you the full lowdown on Scooby and the gang!

MYSTERY INC. FILE

SCOOBY-DOO

Full name: Scoobert-Doo

Nickname: Scooby-Doo, Scoob or Scooby

Age: 49 in dog years (that's 7 in human!)

Height: 12 paws

Address: The Kennel, Shaggy's backyard, Coolsville

Key skills: Speaking. And his long tail allows him to pick the locks of spooky castles and haunted mansions that need investigating!

Likes: Scooby Snacks!

Dislikes: Hunger. Oh, and ghosts and ghouls

Often heard to say: "Rokay!"

DID YOU KNOW?

Shaggy can spin a pizza on his finger like it's a basketball!

MYSTERY INC. FILE

SHAGGY

Full name: Norville Rogers

Nickname: Shaggy

Age: 17 **Height:** 6'0"

Address: 224 Maple Street, Coolsville

Key skills: Shaggy is the master of escape when there is a ghoul around! He even carries a pair of scissors in his back pocket so he can cut himself free if a ghost or villain grabs him!

Likes: Er, food and erm, well, more food

Dislikes: Anything scary!

Often heard to say: "How about a snack, Scoob?"

DID YOU KNOW?

If a creepy ghost or ghoul creeps up on Scooby while he's sleeping, his ears will tap his head to wake him up!

Did you know?

Fred aspires to be a crime writer when he leaves Mystery Inc. He's certainly had enough mystery-solving experience!

MYSTERY INC. FILE

FRED

Full name: Fred Jones

Nickname: Freddie

Age: 16 **Height:** 5'11"

Address: 123 Tuna Lane, Coolsville

Key skills: Building monster traps. He is pretty skilled with a lasso.

Likes: Being in the limelight and reading books

Dislikes: Being tricked by a crook or villain!

Often heard to say: "That wraps up this mystery!"

MYSTERY INC. FILE

DAPHNE

Full name: Daphne Blake

Nickname: Danger Prone Daphne

Age: 16 **Height:** 5'7"

Address: 9000 Easy Street, Coolsville

Key skills: Accidentally discovering secret passages and doorways

Likes: A mystery to solve

Dislikes: Being the damsel in distress

Often heard to say: "Jeepers!"

Did you Know?

When Velma leaves Mystery Inc., she wants to work as a scientist for NASA. That's literally out of this world!

MYSTERY INC. FILE

VELMA

Full name: Velma Dinkley

Nickname: She doesn't have one!

Age: 16 **Height:** 4'9"

Address: 316 Circle Drive, Coolsville

Key skills: Crime solving, lock picking, dusting for fingerprints, and she can speak every language in the world!

Likes: A mystery that challenges her intellect

Dislikes: Losing her glasses!

Often heard to say: "Oh no, my glasses!"

Did you know?

Although Daphne has yet to master riding a bike, she can fly a helicopter! Now that puts a spin on things!

PRIMO PUZZLERS

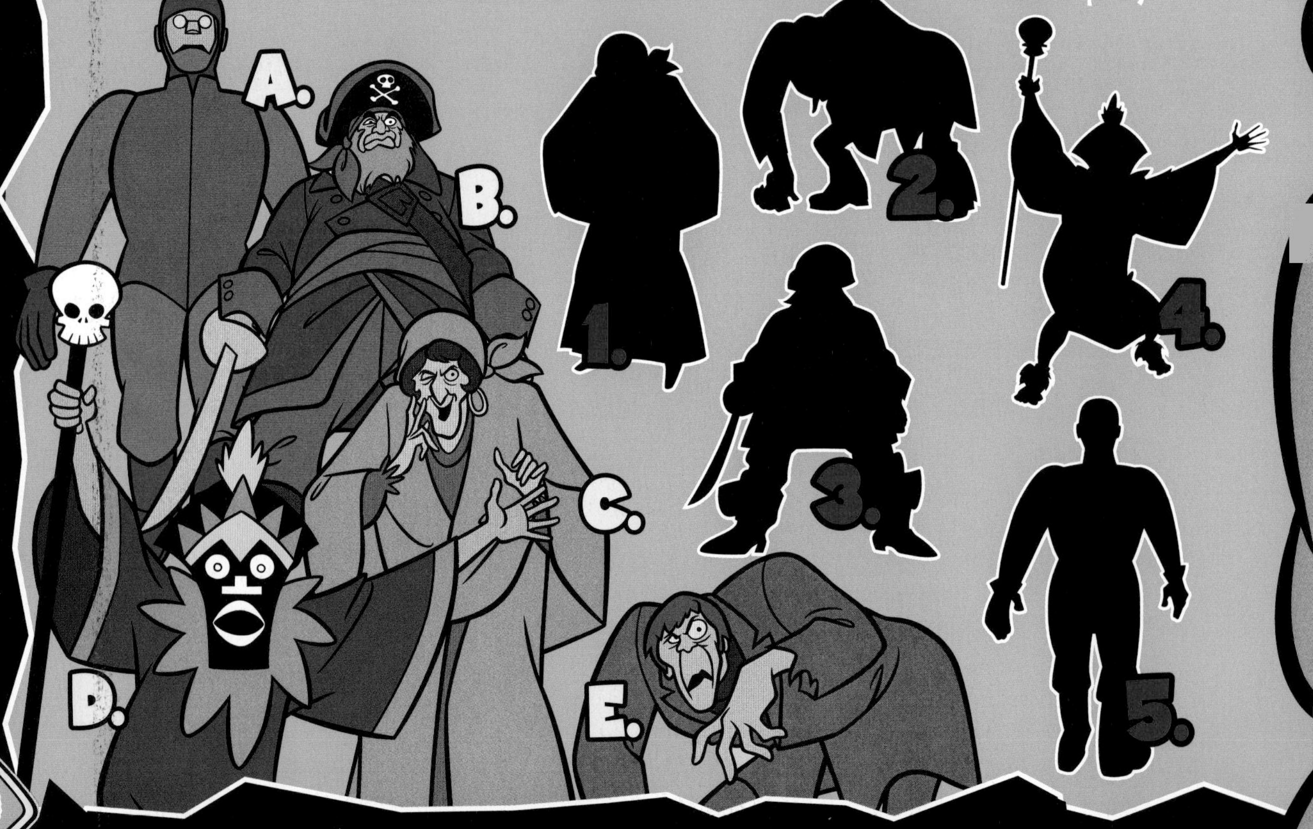

HOP TO IT
CAN YOU SPOT THE SEVEN DIFFERENCES IN THIS SCENE?
SCOOBY SAYS!
DRAW LINES TO MATCH EACH WORD UP WITH ITS OTHER HALF TO SPELL OUT SOME FAMOUS SCOOBY PHRASES!
PESKY
SCOOBY
MY
MYSTERY
FUNLAND
MACHINE
ROBOT
SNACKS
KIDS
GLASSES
Answers:
Loony Letters: Ice cream.
Creepy Crooks: A5, B3, C1, D4, E2.
Hop to It: 1. Square 1 is blue; 2. Square 4 reads
5; 3. Leg spot missing; 4. Bone missing;
5. Foot pad is black; 6. Tail missing; 7. 'D' is
missing from Scooby's collar.
Scooby Says: Pesky kids, Scooby snacks, My
glasses, Mystery Machine, Funland Robot.
11

SPOOK SPOTTER

Mystery Inc. is investigating a seriously haunted house, and they need YOUR help to spot all the spooks! Can you find them all?

Answers on page 156.

Answer on page 156.

OUTER SPACE SCOOBY
Grab your crayons and add some color to this outer space adventure!
28
Hee Hee!

JOIN THE GANG
Discover your Scooby style with this crazy quiz.
1 It's your birthday. What do you ask for?
a) A stylish sweater
b) A new magnifying glass
c) A comfy beanbag
d) A monster-zapping machine
2 There is a mystery you need to solve. A headless horseman is galloping into Coolsville Bank and stealing bags of gold coins! What's the first thing you do?
a) Tremble with fear and eat a burger to calm your nerves
b) Grab your mystery-solving kit
c) Suggest a team meeting to work out the best plan
d) Jump in the Mystery Machine and go, go, go!
SCOOBY SNACKS
5 The Mystery Machine gets a flat tire right outside a spooky graveyard. What do you do?
a) Give Fred a hand repairing it
b) Hop out and ask that nice man if he can help. Hang on, that nice man is really a zombie. Jeepers!
c) Use your cell phone to call for help
d) You grab your roller skates and get out of there as quick as you can
6 What are you most spooked by?
a) Creepy crawlies
b) Ghastly ghosts
c) Nothing spooks you
d) Spooky fog—it makes your hair go frizzy
7 What's your favorite color?
a) Blue
b) Purple
c) Orange
d) Brown

Are you scared like Shaggy or daring like Daphne?

3 **The Mystery Inc. hotline is ringing! Someone needs your help with a mystery! Whaddya do?**

a) Grab the phone and say, "Hello! Got a ghost? We'll be right there!"
b) Stuff your fingers in your ears, shout, "La-la-laaaa!" and pretend you can't hear it
c) Get a notepad and pen so you can write down all the details about the mystery
d) Answer with a polite greeting

KNOCK KNOCK

4 **A knock on the front door makes you jump. Who do you think it is?**

a) It might be a monster, so you ignore it just in case
b) Old Mrs. Grimble from next door
c) Hopefully a werewolf!
d) The pizza delivery man

8 **The cotton candy monster is chasing you through a haunted house. What do you do to escape?**

a) You spot a hidden trap door and jump through it
b) You jump inside a suit of armor
c) You keep running toward the trap you have set up to catch that mad monster
d) You grab a sample of the cotton candy for evidence and then shout to your pals for help

HOW DID YOU DO?

1. a) 3 b) 1 c) 5 d) 10   2. a) 5 b) 1 c) 3 d) 10
3. a) 10 b) 5 c) 1 d) 3   4. a) 3 b) 1 c) 10 d) 5
5. a) 1 b) 3 c) 10 d) 5   6. a) 1 b) 5 c) 10 d) 3
7. a) 10 b) 3 c) 1 d) 5   8. a) 3 b) 5 c) 10 d) 1

1–15 points VELMA'S BUD!

You have got just what it takes to be a top sleuth like Velma! Clever, fast-thinking and with nerves of steel, you are a great addition to the crew!

16–29 points DAPHNE'S FRIEND

You are a valuable addition to the gang because you are smart, brave and full of good ideas. Sometimes you can be too trusting and fall into traps, but you have great pals who always help you out.

30–44 points SHAGGY'S DUDE

Just like Shaggy and Scooby you are ready to run when something spooky is in the air! The mere mention of a monster makes you tremble like jelly, but a bit of light snacking gets you through any sticky situation!

45 or more points FRED'S PAL

Fearless and fun, that's you! You have a lot in common with Freddie and you are never afraid to be first in line for an adventure. Those screaming spooks had better watch out!

SPOOK SPOTTER
The gang has traveled to the bottom of a freak-infested lake!
Can you help them spot all the watery weirdos?

Answers on page 156.

Mystery Stink
The gang had a close shave with The Creep at his swamp! They escaped but are covered in mud! Can you figure out who's who?
1
2
3
4
5
Answers: 1. Daphne; 2. Shaggy; 3. Fred; 4. Velma; 5. Scooby.

YOU'VE BEEN FRAMED

CRIME SCENE•CRIME SCENE•

The Witch Doctor's changed this crime photo to make it look like SCOOBY stole the ancient amulet! Can you find five things he's changed?

CRIME SCENE•CRIME SC

Answers: 1. "Scooby did it" on the wall. 2. Scooby Snacks. 3. Amulet has moved. 4. Burglar mask. 5. Footprints.

GROOVY GAMES
HEADS UP
It's not just the Headless Horseman that's losing his head! Can you match each villain with its head?
1
2
3
4
5
A
B
C
D
E
BOO!
The gang was so afraid of a ghost that they ran through a fence! Can you work out who made which hole?
1
2
3
4
5

Answers on page 156.

Scary Shadows

Velma needs all of her detective skills to match up each of these scary shadows with its owner! Can you help her match them up?

Answers: 1E, 2J, 3H, 4D, 5F, 6I, 7G, 8B, 9C, 10A.

TREASURE ISLAND
Scooby-Doo and the gang are hot on the heels of Captain Redbeard. Can you unscramble this message and discover the buried treasure before he does?
A B C D E F
G H I J K L
M N O P Q
R S T U V X
Y Z
Answer: The treasure chest is next to the tall palm tree.

MYSTERY MAYHEM
THROUGH THE KEYHOLE
Shaggy's too afraid to look through the keyhole to see who's outside!
Can you work out who–or what–is through each hole?
A
B
C
D
SNACK ATTACK
Follow the lines to spell one of Scooby's favorite snacks!
O
G
O
T
H
D

A forger has made a copy of this priceless painting. Can you help Velma find five mistakes the forger made?

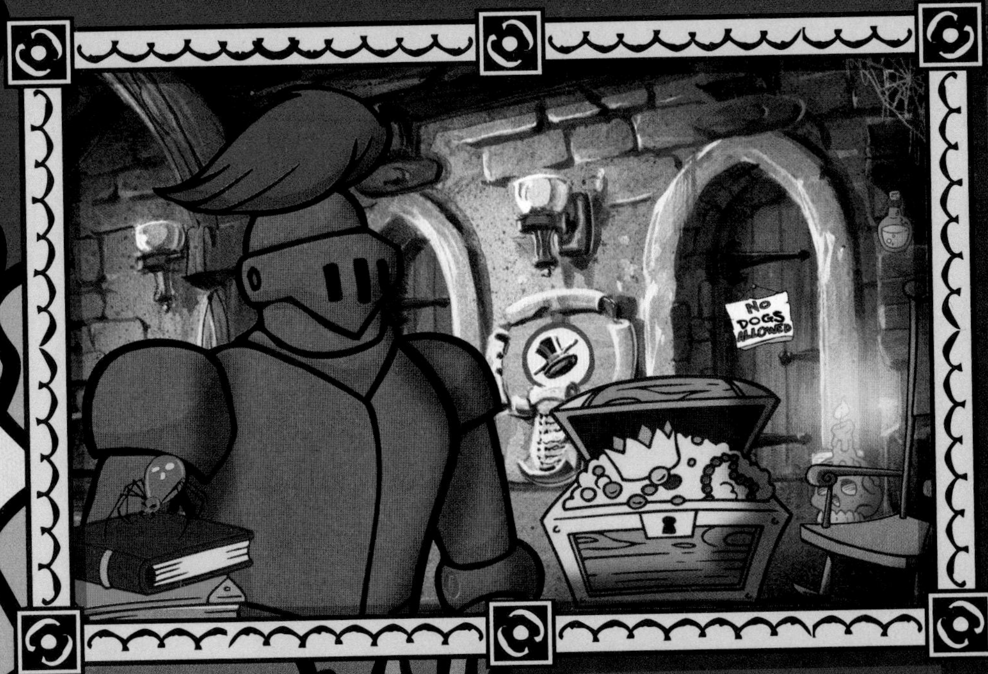

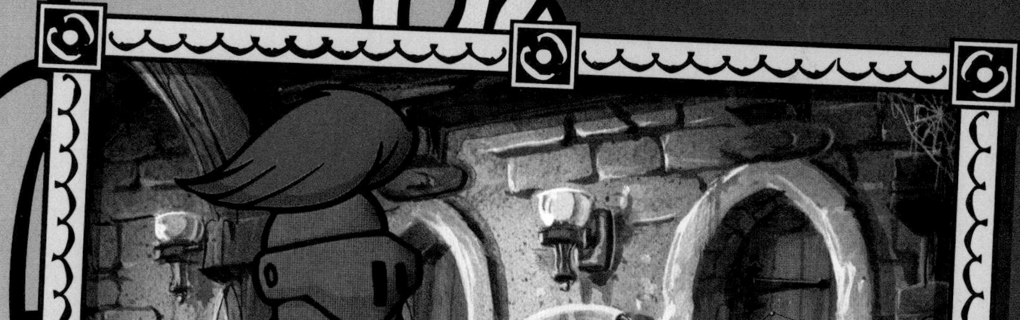

Answers:

Through the Keyhole: A. Daphne; B. Scooby; C. The Creep; D. Fred.

Snack Attack: Hot dog.

Detective Skills: 1. Potion; 2. Jewels in treasure chest; 3. Spider; 4. Knight's helmet; 5. Door behind the knight.

Wish you were here!

MINE
GET YOUR OWN
WOLF CROSSING
OLD MILL
BEAR HUGS 50¢
SILAS LONG
MISTER BONE JANGLES
WASH 'N WEARWOLF DYED 1980
THE MYSTERY MACHINE
POISON IVY RELIEF
CONE SWEET CONE
NURSERY
CREEPY CREEK

SPOOK SPOTTER

The gang is trapped in a haunted graveyard! Can you spot all the dangers to help them find a safe way out?

Answers on page 156.

PRIMO PUZZLERS

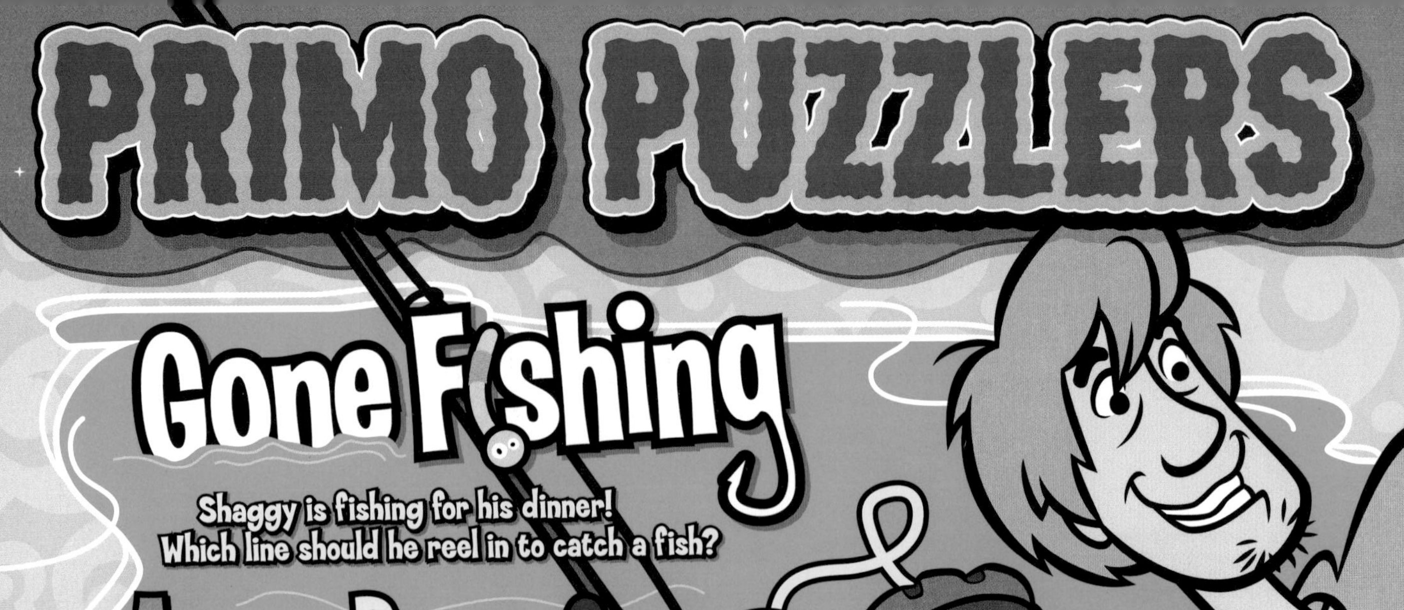

Gone Fishing

Shaggy is fishing for his dinner! Which line should he reel in to catch a fish?

BOOK WORM

Velma has a huge collection of books! Can you match each stack of books with its shadow?

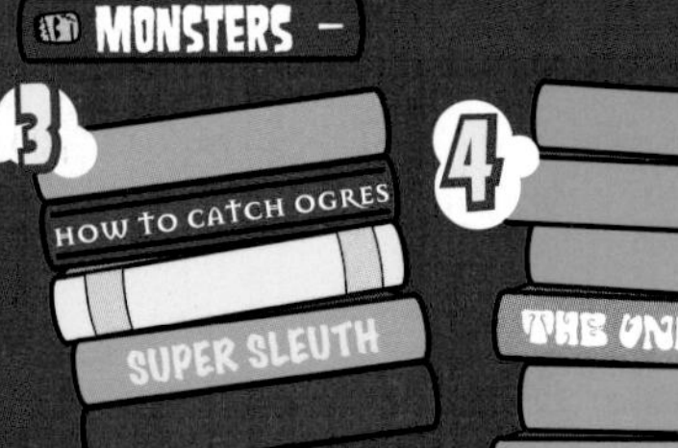

MYSTERY TOUR
Mystery Inc. has solved crimes all over the world. Can you fit the places they have traveled into this grid?
DUBLIN
LOCH NESS
INDIA
SWEDEN
VENICE
EGYPT
LONDON
PARIS
MEXICO
HAWAII
Answers:
Gone Fishing: Line C.
Book Worm: 1E, 2D, 3A, 4C, 5F, 6B.
Mystery Tour: Across: London, Mexico, India, Venice, Paris;
Down: Sweden, Loch Ness, Hawaii, Dublin, Egypt.

MYSTERY MAYHEM

This Scooby-Doo mystery has gotten scrambled! Can you put it back in the correct order so that it makes sense?

D "Well I guess that wraps up this mystery!" says Fred. "Well done Scooby, your hungry tummy has helped us to solve this mystery!"

B "Hello. It's Mr. Slice. I have a ghost wreaking havoc in my bakery. All my customers are terrified. Can you help?"

I . . . but the cake stand wobbles and knocks down the whole row of cakes!

A As the gang discusses the mystery, Scooby starts sniffing around the nearest cake stand when suddenly the ghost appears! Everyone runs for cover.

G "Yuck! You meddling kids! I'm covered in custard!" shouts the ghost.

H Scooby is scared of the ghost, but he can't resist the cakes! He grabs the nearest cake . . .

K Mr. Slice explains the problem to the gang. The ghost appears every day at lunchtime. It appears from behind the counter in a cloud of flour.

C A large custard pie wobbles and then falls–Splat!–right on top of the ghost!

J "Why, it's Mr. Suet from the cake shop down the road!" says Mr. Slice. "Call the police!"

F "You are doomed! These cakes are mine. Leave this shop forever!" shrieks the ghost.

E Early one morning, the Mystery Inc. hotline starts ringing. Fred answers it and says, "Hello, Mystery Inc. How can we help?"

L Fred puts the phone down, and the gang sets off to investigate.

THE CORRECT ORDER IS:

	B					H					

Answer: The correct order is E, B, L, K, A, F, H, I, C, G, J, D.

GHOST BUSTERS

Can you work out the hidden question that these spooks are trying to ask the gang?

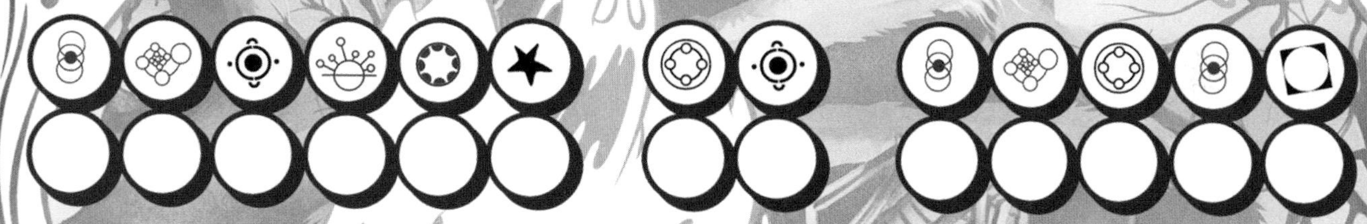

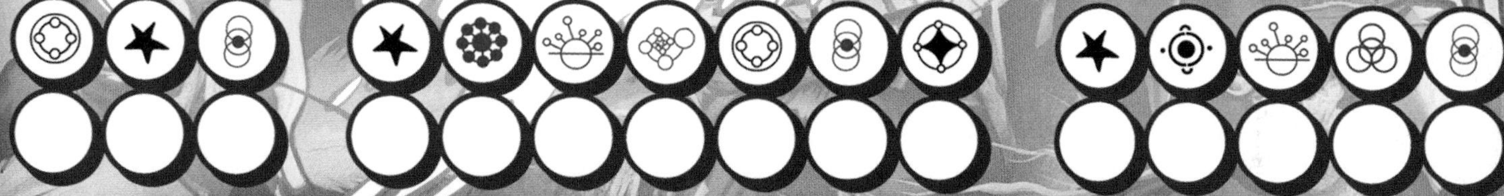

Answer: Are you brave enough to enter the haunted house?

GROOVY GAMES

Point the finger!

Velma is busy doing some detective work with these fingerprints! Can you help her match each one with its twin?

ICE SCREAM

Shaggy is buying an ice cream but that mean old Cotton Candy Monster has mixed up all the flavors! Help Shaggy to unscramble each flavor.

A LCTOCEOAH

B NBANAA

C NGMOA

D CKOEOIS NDA MCREA

E ALUNAIL

F UTTTI RTFIIU

GRID LOCKED
H
H
G
G
V
E
Give Fred a hand rounding up these villains and fitting them into the grid. Use the letters already in the grid as clues.
ALIEN (5)
HAG (3)
GHOST (5)
WITCH (5)
BIG FOOT (3, 4)
MONSTER (7)
GREMLIN (7)
VAMPIRE (7)
HaHa!
When is it bad luck to meet a black cat?
When you're a mouse!
Why was there a fence around the graveyard?
Because people were dying to get in!
HaHa!
Hee Hee!
HaHa!
Answers:
Point the Finger: 1F, 2D, 3A, 4B, 5E, 6C.
Ice Scream: A. Chocolate; B. Banana; C. Mango; D. Cookies and cream; E. Vanilla; F. Tutti Fruiti.
Ice Scream: Across: Witch, Alien, Monster, Vampire;
Down: Ghost, Hag, Bigfoot, Gremlin.

THE SPOOK SPOTTER FILES
When you go ghost hunting, don't forget to take your Spook Spotter Files. They are just what you need to identify monsters and work out how to catch them. The first file reveals all about vampires.
PART ONE
Vampires
1 2 3 4 5 6 7 8 9 10
Shaggy's Scare-o-meter
Like, vampires are totally scary, it's official!
If you bump into one of these blood-suckers, you should say, "Hello, Mr. Vampire. Would you like some garlic soup?" and then run, run, run!
BLOOD
TRANSYLVANIA
Villain Checklist:
Does the suspect have:
DO NOT DISTURB
Fangs
A pet bat
A creepy cape
A coffin to sleep in
A fear of sunlight
VELMA'S VERDICT
Any crook can transform himself into a vampire. Take a cape, some fake fangs and a well-trained pet bat, and the illusion is complete. The surefire way to spot if your vampire is a phony is if you find a bag of strawberry candy in its pocket. Why? Strawberry candy is the perfect way to get the effect of bloodstained teeth! Simple!
38

Eye Spy

Test your spy skills by finding 10 differences between these two scary scenes!

Answers: 1. Monster's eye color; 2. Bat; 3. Werewolf's jacket; 4. Burger; 5. Spider's dot; 6. Money bag; 7. Zombie's hair; 8. Frog; 9. Mummy's missing; 10. Top hat.

Check off each time you spy a change!

Mystery Inc.'s latest case has taken them to Ancient Egypt where an angry mummy is wreaking havoc. Help the gang to wrap up this mummy mystery!

Scooby and Shaggy are lost inside a pyramid! Can you help Velma find them without bumping into spooky mummies?

Fred's Facts

Find out some crazy-but-true facts about the ancient Egyptians!

The largest pyramid is called the Great Pyramid. It was built in 2600 B.C. for Pharaoh Khufu, and it took hundreds of men more than 20 years to build!

Hieroglyphics is a special language using pictures instead of letters. The ancient Egyptians invented it, and they used it to write on the walls of tombs and temples.

The ancient Egyptians believed that mummification allowed them to live forever. The dead body would be washed and wrapped in linen strips. Amulets (magic charms) would be placed between the strips to protect the mummy in the afterlife. Spooky!

Pyramids were built as tombs for the pharaohs of ancient Egypt.

The ancient Egyptians believed that onions kept evil spirits away.

Answers on page 157.

SECRET SIGNS

The gang has discovered a picture message on the wall of the pyramid, but they need to unravel the code to understand what it says! Can you help them?

OH MUMMY

The mummy is hiding in one of these caskets, but Velma can't figure out which one! Follow the clues to work it out!

1. THE MUMMY IS HIDING BELOW A CASKET WITH A BIRD ON IT.
2. IT IS ABOVE A CASKET WITH A GREEN CAT.
3. THE MUMMY DOESN'T LIKE RED STRIPES.

Keep Your Eyes Peeled
Use your detective skills to tackle this brain game!
Study the scene for one minute and
then cover the page up.
Now it's time to answer the questions on the right!
JAM
SCOOBY SNACKS

Answers: 1. A; 2. C; 3. B; 4. B; 5. False; 6. A; 7. A; 8. A; 9. B; 10. False.

Clean Machine

The gang loves nothing more than to give the Mystery Machine a good old scrub! Can you solve this picture puzzler?

a

b

c

d

1 2 3 4 5 6

Find the image in the picture above and record the grid reference in the box below! Here's an example!

1

2

3

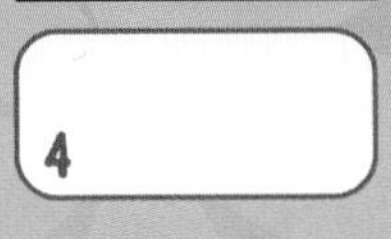

4

5

6

Answers: 1 b-6; 2 a-3; 3 c-2; 4 b-3; 5 b-5; 6 c-4.

Scooby's Snack Attack

Scooby-Doo is a real hungry hound! Help him to track down all of these tasty snacks hidden in the grid.

C	I	Y	O	M	E	L	E	T	B	T	S
B	O	E	A	P	P	L	E	P	I	E	C
M	H	O	T	D	O	G	O	N	B	W	O
T	F	P	K	P	Y	I	M	N	E	S	O
Y	C	O	W	I	Q	P	I	U	B	E	B
W	E	P	H	Z	E	A	L	F	F	E	Y
A	A	S	O	Z	E	S	K	S	C	D	S
[illegible]	N	I	N	A	X	T	S	I	A	X	N
R	A	D	P	E	J	A	H	T	K	S	A
E	N	C	H	I	P	S	A	M	E	L	C
J	A	P	A	B	C	S	K	B	O	A	K
O	B	U	R	G	E	R	E	P	O	C	S

SCOOBY SNACKS CAKE PASTA PIZZA
OMELET CHIPS BANANA BURGER
HOT DOG APPLE PIE MILKSHAKE COOKIES

Answers on page 157.

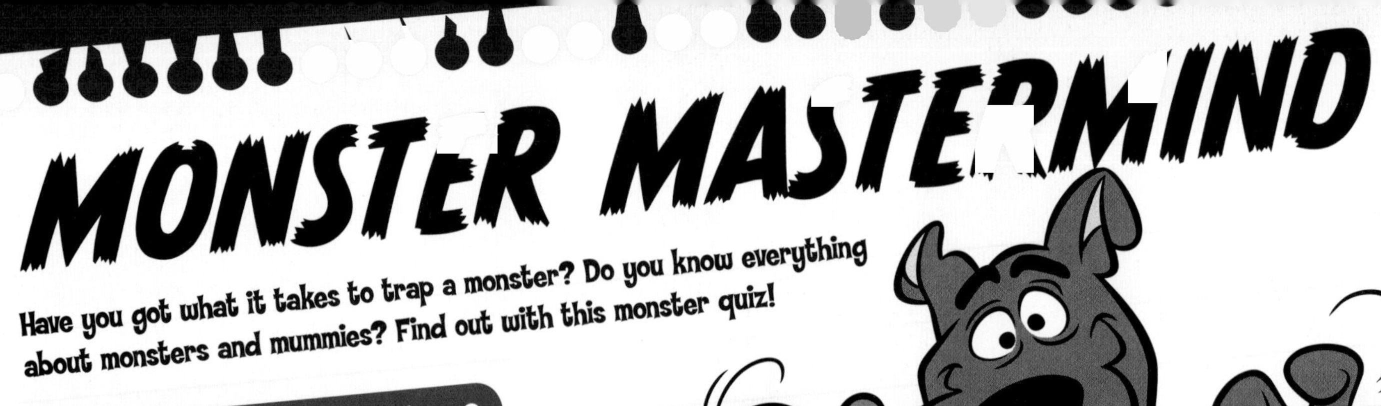

MONSTER MASTERMIND

Have you got what it takes to trap a monster? Do you know everything about monsters and mummies? Find out with this monster quiz!

1. Which of these is not a ghost?
a) Phantom b) Zombie c) Poltergeist

2. Folklore says that witches and ghouls come out to play on what special night of the year?

3. What does UFO stand for?
a) Unusually Furry Orangutan
b) Unidentified Flying Object
c) Ugly Freaky Object

4. What kind of spook usually owns a black cat?
a) A tar monster
b) A vampire
c) A witch

5. True or false: Zombies are also known as the living dead.

T F

6. What kind of creepy creature can you scare away with garlic?
a) A vampire b) A werewolf c) A mummy

7. What is the word for spooky goings-on and weird creepiness?
a) Supernatural
b) Superscary
c) Superspooky

8. What is another name for a yeti?
a) The Astonishing Snow Creature
b) The Amazing Snow Beast
c) The Abominable Snowman

9. True or false: Werewolves are half wolf, half tiger.

HOW DID YOU DOO?

Once you have completed the quiz, check your answers below. Award yourself a Scooby Snack for each correct answer and then discover your monster-mashing ability!

1. B
2. Halloween, October 31
3. B
4. C
5. True
6. A
7. Supernatural
8. C
9. False—werewolves are half wolf, half human!

1-3 SNACKS—FREAKY FEAR!

You get spooked by anything freaky, and Scooby and Shaggy think you are, like, totally right! Monsters should be avoided at all costs!

4-6 SNACKS—FEARLESS FUN!

Monsters don't scare you, and you love reading ghoulish stories! If you were to bump into a scary, creepy creature, you'd know just what to do!

7-9 SNACKS—MONSTER MAD!

Scooberific! You really know your monster stuff! Velma is very impressed by your ghoulish knowledge.

Mystery Inc. could use a monster masher like you!

Dog's Dinner

Can you help Scooby-Doo find his dinner before he faints from hunger?

SCOOBY

START

1

2

3

Answer: Path 2.

Clued Up

DISH OF THE DAY

Like, I'm starving, man! Can you pair the food on the left with the food on the right to create some delicious dishes?

1 STRAWBERRIES	A EGGS
2 BACON	B POTATOES
3 BURGERS	C DUMPLINGS
4 STEAK	D CREAM
5 CHICKEN	E FRIES

1 ☐ 2 ☐ 3 ☐ 4 ☐ 5 ☐

FIND YER FEET

These characters have got their feet mixed up and it's toe-tal chaos! Can you match each pair of feet to its owner?

A B C D

1

2

3

4

Answers:
Dish of the Day: 1D, 2A, 3E, 4B, 5C.
Find Yer Feet: A4, B3, C2, D1.

He's Batty: Bats, green, witch, scream, Velma, machine.
The answer is garlic.
What a Sweetie: D.

HE'S BATTY
Count Dracula has trapped Daphne in a spooky dungeon! The only way to open the door and free her is to solve these clues and use the letters in the yellow boxes to complete the grid.
These flying creatures are a vampire's best friend
2
The color of Shaggy's t-shirt
1
A spooky old hag who owns a cauldron and a black cat
5
The loud noise you make when something makes you jump
3
The only member of the gang who wears glasses
4
The gang drives around in a van called the Mystery ________
6
1
2
3
4
5
6
WHAT A SWEETIE
Can you work out which jar of candy matches the one in the picture?
A
B
C
D
E
F

SPOOK SPOTTER
The gang is on a top-secret undercover mission, but they have been ambushed by spy monsters! Can you help spot all the spooks?

Answers on page 157.

PICTURE PUZZLE

Write the name of each object in the grid to reveal one of the gang's favorite places.

1
2
3
4
5
6
7
8
9
10

CLUES!

1 2 3 4 5
6 7 8 9 10

Answers: 1. Ice cream; 2. Ghost; 3. Book; 4. Cauldron; 5. Milkshake; 6. Television; 7. Vampire; 8. Umbrella; 9. Balloon; 10. Cake. Hidden word: Coolsville.

SHADOW SPOOKS

These spooky shadows are making poor Scooby-Doo tremble with fear! Can you work out what each shadow belongs to?

A B C
D E F G
H I J

Which two items don't have matching pairs?

Answers: A-12; B-11; C-3; D-5; E-9; F-10; G-7; H-1; I-8; J-2.
Missing pairs: 4 and 6.

Clued Up

Knight Fright
SD
Can you figure out who is hiding inside each spooky suit of armor?
A
B
C
D
A
B
C
D
BREAKING UP
Like, oops! Shaggy has dropped Velma's magnifying glass! Can you work out which piece is needed to put it back together again?
A
B
C
D

Answers:
Knight Fright: a. Shaggy; b. Fred; c. The Gypsy; d. Dracula.
Breaking Up: B.
Sporty Scooby: Golf; Basketball; Football; Surfing; Tennis; Jumping rope. Hidden Sports: Baseball, Frisbee.

WHO ARE YOU IN THE SCOOBY CREW?

Are you a groovy dude like Shaggy, or a super-sleuthing brainiac like Velma?

Take this quiz to find out!

1 What do you like to do in your spare time?

a) Shop 'til you drop and spend time with your pals
b) Kick back on a beanbag with some Scooby Snacks
c) Read a book about mysteries and get top tips on sleuthing
d) Head outside for a game of high-speed tag with your friends

2 The Mystery Inc. kids are famous for their groovy Scooby styles! What look would you choose?

a) A fabulous coordinated outfit with cool accessories
b) Hippy chic with a funky t-shirt and flares
c) A sensible outfit topped off with a cool pair of glasses
d) Dressy pants and a top complete with a fun neckerchief for a splash of color

3 There's a spook hiding out in a cellar, and it's up to you to go and catch it! Whaddya say?

a) It sounds kinda spooky, but I'll give it a try!
b) Like, nope, no way and never ever! Spooky cellars are so not my thing!
c) Hmm, this could be a fantastic opportunity to investigate a spook up close.
d) Sure! I'll teach that goony ghoul a thing or two!

4 While you are investigating the spooky cellar, you hear a ghoulish giggle. What do you think it is?

a) It's just one of the gang playing a trick on me.
b) L-l-like, it's gotta be the Giggling Green Ghost! I'm outta here!
c) My Giggle Analysis Machine says that it is a fake spook, and I have nothing to be scared of!
d) Pah! I'm not afraid of anything that giggles!

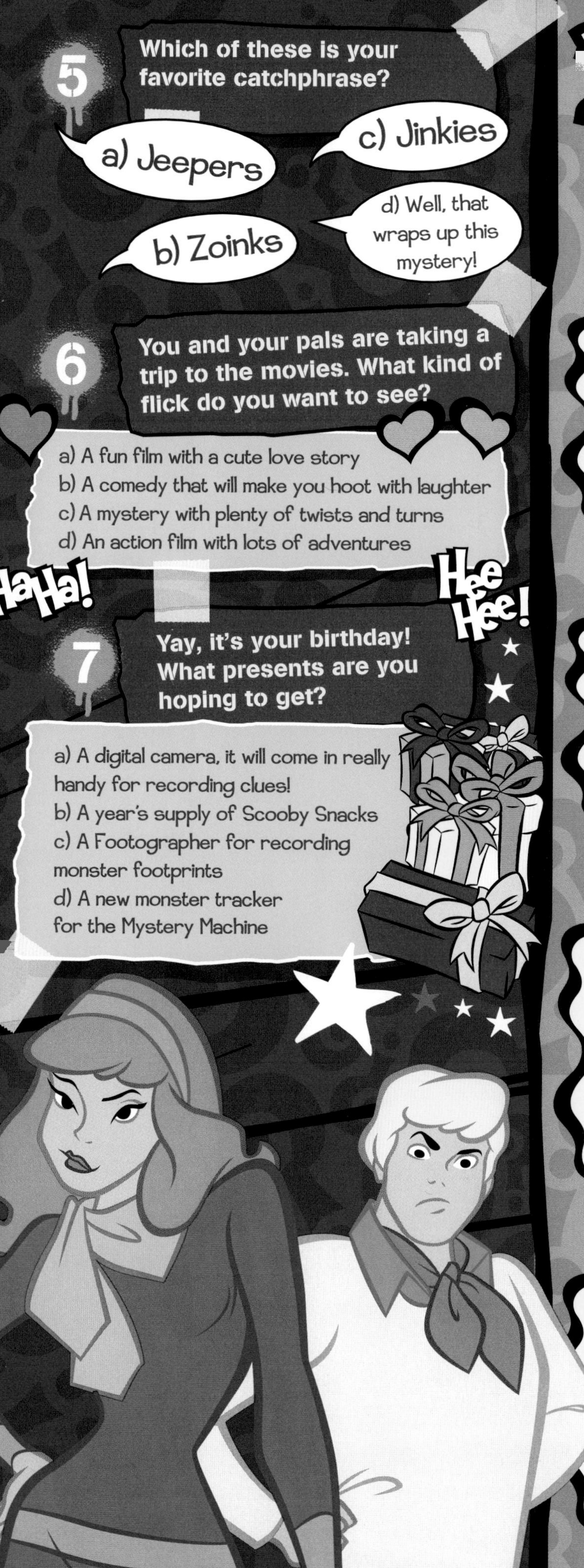

5 Which of these is your favorite catchphrase?

a) Jeepers
b) Zoinks
c) Jinkies
d) Well, that wraps up this mystery!

6 You and your pals are taking a trip to the movies. What kind of flick do you want to see?

a) A fun film with a cute love story
b) A comedy that will make you hoot with laughter
c) A mystery with plenty of twists and turns
d) An action film with lots of adventures

7 Yay, it's your birthday! What presents are you hoping to get?

a) A digital camera, it will come in really handy for recording clues!
b) A year's supply of Scooby Snacks
c) A Footographer for recording monster footprints
d) A new monster tracker for the Mystery Machine

How Did You DOO?

Mostly As

You and Daphne would get along just great! You both love solving mysteries and you like to do it with style. Just like Daphne you make a great team player, and you will always try your best to help your friends out of sticky situations!

Mostly Bs

Like, whoa! You have got soo much in common with Shaggy and the Scoobster! You love to have fun, and your best buds are really important to you. Spooky stuff isn't really your thing, but throw in a few tasty treats and you'll be there!

Mostly Cs

Velma reckons you would make a top detective! You are thoughtful, hardworking and dedicated, just like Velma. Your amazing brainpower has helped you out of lots of difficult positions. Sometimes you can get a bit spooked, but you always find a logical solution for any mysterious situation!

Mostly Ds

Well, Fred reckons you've got what it takes to solve mysteries and mash monsters! You are totally brave, and no monster has beaten you yet! You love to succeed, but you know your success is all down to your brilliant team of pals. Those monsters and ghouls had better watch out!

Crack the Clues

Use your ace detective skills to solve this creepy crossword.

ACROSS

1. Velma's favorite word (7)
3. If a ghost lives in a house, it is said to be this (7)
8. The town where the gang lives (10)
9. The country where mummies and pyramids are found (5)
11. Fruit used to make Halloween lanterns (7)
13. Bird that comes out at night (3)
14. Scooby's favorite kind of treat (6, 6)
15. The member of the gang who wears blue pants (4)

DOWN

2. A spook made of bones (8)
4. Creatures from another planet (6)
5. A scary, hairy type of spider (9)
6. Scooby is a Great ---- (4)
7. Another name for a yeti (7)
10. Witches cast these (6)
12. Loch Ness is home to one of these (7)

Answers: Across: 1. Jinkies; 3. Haunted; 8. Coolsville; 9. Egypt; 11. Pumpkin; 13. Owl; 14. Scooby Snacks; 15. Fred. Down: 2. Skeleton; 4. Aliens; 5. Tarantula; 6. Dane; 7. Bigfoot; 10. Spells; 12. Monster.

MYSTERY MAKEOVER
Dracula has given the Mystery Machine a makeover! Can you find the 10 crazy changes he's made?
THE MYSTERY MACHINE
THE MENACE MACHINE
Check a box each time you see a change!
Answers: 1. Flame; 2. Skull; 3. The Menace Machine; 4. Red seats; 5. Bat on front; 6. Roof bar missing; 7. Steering wheel; 8. Exhaust; 9. Spider web; 10. Bumper.

ZOINKS!

Mystery Inc. has discovered a spooky Egyptian tomb. Can you find all the objects in this creepy pyramid puzzler?

CHECK OFF AS YOU FIND . . .

- 4 Camels ______
- 2 Yellow snakes ______
- A mummified cat ______
- 3 Herons ______
- 3 Hungry alligators ______
- A buried mummy ______
- A mummified snake ______
- An alligator hieroglyph ______
- All 5 members of Mystery Inc. ______

Answers on page 157.

THE KING'S CHAMBER

THE TREASURE ROOM

ALLIGATOR POOL

A GREAT PYRAMID
reeeee!
TRAPDOOR
SECRET PASSAGES
Paul Gamble
boing!
SECRET STAIRWELL TO THE TOMB
SNAKE PIT

Scooby Search

Mystery Inc. needs your help! They must find all the words listed below in the grid. The words are hidden horizontally, vertically, backward, forward and diagonally.

F	R	O	T	C	O	D	H	C	T	I	W
W	I	B	K	R	V	B	Y	L	O	R	Y
E	O	N	O	I	X	A	T	U	C	Y	M
N	L	D	G	M	V	I	T	E	P	E	M
I	A	Z	M	E	H	R	E	A	G	S	U
H	R	M	U	Q	R	E	W	R	X	U	M
C	Z	S	D	R	S	P	T	O	E	O	A
A	M	W	J	U	R	E	R	A	L	H	E
M	V	R	I	I	M	E	A	I	B	D	V
Y	I	H	N	O	K	R	P	K	N	E	I
R	L	T	K	J	T	C	D	Z	G	T	T
E	L	L	I	V	S	L	O	O	C	N	C
T	A	S	E	D	X	W	O	I	Z	U	E
S	I	T	S	A	T	M	R	N	Y	A	T
Y	N	K	G	H	O	U	L	K	R	H	E
M	O	N	S	T	E	R	S	S	R	V	D

- ☐ Mystery Machine
- ☐ Clue
- ☐ Creeper
- ☐ Haunted House
- ☐ Mudman
- ☐ Ghoul
- ☐ Monsters
- ☐ Jinkies
- ☐ Witch Doctor
- ☐ Detective
- ☐ Fingerprint
- ☐ Mummy
- ☐ Zoinks
- ☐ Scooby Snacks
- ☐ Crime
- ☐ Trapdoor
- ☐ Coolsville
- ☐ Pawprint
- ☐ Villain

Uh-oh! Shaggy is playing a joke on the gang and has taken one of the words! Can you work out which entry doesn't appear in the grid?

Missing Entry: ____________________

Answers on page 157.

SHADOW SPOOKS

Poor Scooby-Doo is terrified of shadows! Match each object with its shadow so he doesn't feel so spooked!

Answers: 1E; 2C; 3F; 4A; 5H; 6J; 7I; 8B; 9G; 10D.

The Haunted

Mystery Inc. needs your help! The Fantastic Fun Fair is being haunted by a scary spook, and the visitors are being scared away! Solve these clues and help the gang discover who the villain is and where it is hiding!

Which Way Now?

Scooby is going to use his highly sensitive nose to sniff out the first clue. Guide him past the snacks and straight to the clue!

Get the Message

Scooby has brought the clue back to the gang, but it is written in a secret code! Put the first letter of each object in the squares below to find out where the villain is hiding!

Fairground

Picture It

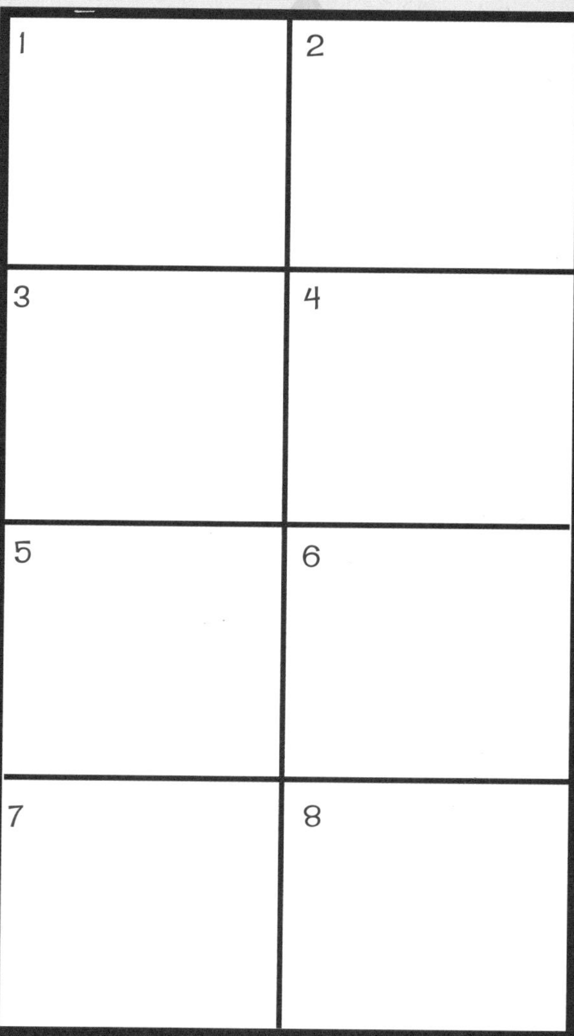

The gang has found the final clue that will reveal the villain's identity! Copy each of the numbered boxes into the grid to expose the spooky troublemaker.

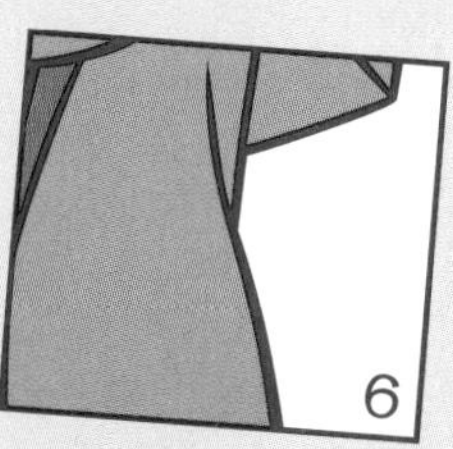

Answers:
Which Way Now?: Path C.
Get the Message: The Ghost Train.
Picture It: The Gypsy.

Answer on page 157.

ANIMAL

Cryptic clues
USE YOUR DETECTIVE SKILLS TO SOLVE THE CLUES AND FIT THE ANSWERS INTO THE GRID.
1.
2.
3.
4.
5.
6.
7.
8.
9.
10.
11.
12.
13.
DOWN
1. A SCOOBY VILLAIN WHO HAUNTS A CIRCUS (5, 5)
2. COLOR OF DAPHNE'S DRESS (6)
3. BLOOD-SUCKING GHOUL (7)
5. SCOOBY WEARS ONE AROUND HIS NECK (6)
9. SCOOBY'S BEST BUD (6)
11. FRED'S LAST NAME (5)
ACROSS
4. A SNACK MADE WITH BREAD AND A FILLING (8)
6. THE GANG COLLECTS THESE TO SOLVE MYSTERIES (5)
7. PLACE WHERE THE GANG LIVES (10)
8. TYPE OF DOG SCOOBY IS: GREAT ---- (4)
10. HAG WHO RIDES A BROOMSTICK (5)
12. SWEET, ROUND SNACK WITH A HOLE IN THE MIDDLE (8)
13. WHEN THE GANG GOES UNDERCOVER, THEY WEAR D-------- SO THAT NOBODY RECOGNIZES THEM (9)
Answers: 1. Ghost Clown; 2. Purple; 3. Vampire; 4. Sandwich; 5. Collar; 6. Clues;
7. Coolsville; 8. Dane; 9. Shaggy; 10. Witch; 11. Jones; 12. Doughnut; 13. Disguises.

THE SPOOK SPOTTER FILES
PART TWO
Aliens
blip blip
blip blip
blip
blip blip
blip blip blip bliiiip!
Villain Checklist:
Does the suspect have:
Antennae
2 heads
Webbed feet
A spaceship
Green, spotty skin
Shaggy's Scare-o-meter
1 2 3 4 5 6 7 8 9 10
Like, aliens are totally creepy. Scoob and I should know. We were once taken aboard a spaceship! But they were friendly, and their space snacks were really tasty, so I reckon they score 5/10 on my Scare-o-meter!
SPACE SNACKS
VELMA'S VERDICT
Usually aliens are just trying to find out more about humans and aren't trying to spook us. Crop circles and mysterious lights in the sky are signs that they are trying to say hello! So if you bump into an alien, talk to it and see what it says. I'm fluent in Alienish so give me a call if you need a hand with translating!

CHECK YOUR FACTS

How well do you know Mystery Inc.? All of these facts are true, but do you know which member of the gang each one is about? Use your super-sleuthing skills to work it out and write your answers in the boxes.
8
My nose is brilliant for sniffing out clues
Name:..
9
WHEN I AM OLDER, I WOULD LIKE TO BE A scientist
Name:..
10
I like to make gadgets and gizmos for trapping MONSTERS.
Name:..
11
I am the oldest member of the gang.
Name:..
12
I am the only gang member who doesn't have a nickname.
Name:..
Answers: 1. Daphne; 2. Shaggy; 3. Velma; 4. Shaggy; 5. Daphne; 6. Fred; 7. Shaggy and Scooby-Doo; 8. Scooby-Doo; 9. Velma; 10. Fred; 11. Shaggy; 12. Velma.
71

Clued Up
Use your super-sleuthing skills to solve these mysteries.
GHOSTBUSTING
G H O S T A G N
H A N T S O H G
O F J P O F O A
S T S O H G S N
T S O H G J T F
Poor Scooby is terrified of ghosts, and there are lots of them hiding in the Mystery Machine. Can you count how many are hiding in the grid?
BARE NECESSITIES
Before the gang sets off to solve another mystery, Shaggy always packs a few supplies! Can you work out which three items he has forgotten?
Shaggy's Diary

CRYPTIC CODES

Check out Fred's new invention, the Code Cracker Extraordinaire 3000! Use it to help you unravel these hidden messages.

FRED'S

Code Cracker Extraordinaire 3000

A B C D
E F G H
I J K L
M N O P
Q R S T
U V W X
ON Y Z OFF

DON'T TOUCH!

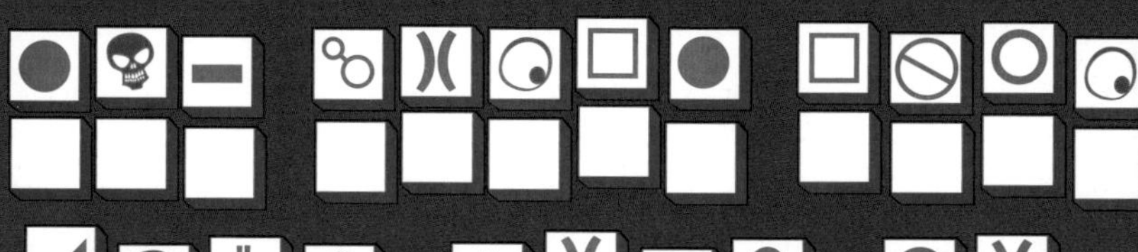

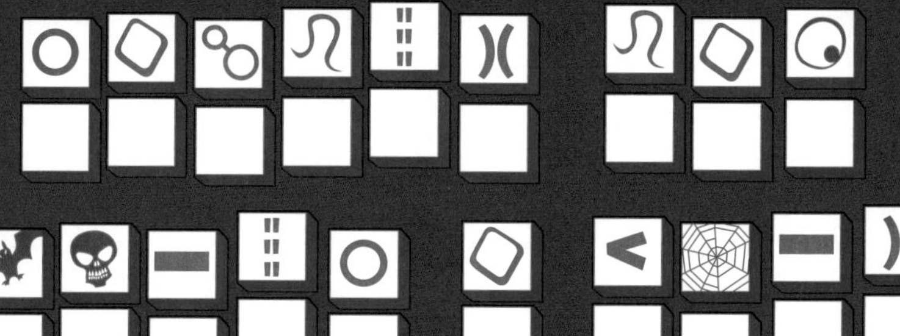

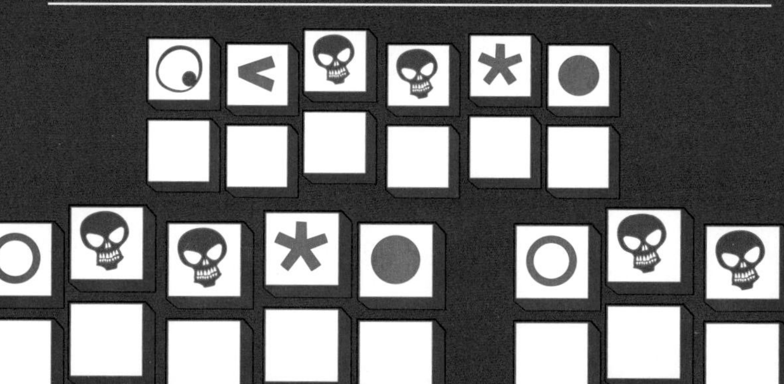

Answers:
Ghostbusting: The word ghost appears seven times.
Bare Necessities: Shaggy has forgotten his diary, a muffin and a Scooby Snack.
Cryptic Codes: How about a snack, Scoob? You pesky kids won't beat me.
Daphne has found a clue. Scooby Dooby Doo.

Super Snackin'
Scooby-Doo and Shaggy are getting ready for a feast of their favorite treats! Can you find all of their favorite snacks hidden in the grid?
S N C H I P S A N B
P A K G C I E M R A
A R N T B Z I G S N
G P H D P Z K B E A
H C P K W A O H K N
E B D L O I O I A A
T K A T E T C P H N
T Z N C D N A H S T
I P T O A G E P K Z
R E G R U B D S L Z
S D O R A N G E I I
L E M O N A D E M P
Cookies
Burger
Orange
Milkshake
Cake
Banana
Sandwich
Pizza
Apple
Spaghetti
Chips
Hot dog
Lemonade
Uh-oh! Scooby has gobbled up one of the snacks! Can you work out which treat is missing from the grid?
Missing snack.......................................
Answers on page 158.
74

WAVE CRAZE

Scooby-Doo is riding the waves like a pro! Can you copy the scene into the grid below before he falls off his surfboard? When you have finished, color him in!

GROOVY GAMES

A PERFECT POSE

Can you match up each of Scooby's poses with its matching pair?

Which pose doesn't have a matching pair?

Get a Clue

How many times can you see the word CLUE hidden in this grid?

C	L	U	E	C	U
L	E	C	U	L	E
U	C	L	L	U	U
E	E	U	C	E	L
U	L	E	U	L	C
E	C	L	U	E	U

SILLY SQUARES
Reveal the Scooby crook by drawing each of the missing squares into the grid to complete the picture.
Answers:
A Perfect Pose: 1E; 2A; 3C; 4F; 6B; 7D; pose 5 doesn't have a matching pair.
Get a Clue: "Clue" appears eight times.
Silly Squares: The Wolfman.
77

Which member of Mystery Inc. are you most like? Take the quiz below to find out!

You receive a call saying that a mysterious, ghostly mummy is causing mayhem at the Museum of Ancient Egypt. Your help is urgently needed! Do you:

a) Head for the Mystery Machine and jump behind the wheel
b) Stop first to pack a suitcase. Well, you need to look your best!
c) Grab your notebook and get going
d) Finish your dinner first

☐

You arrive at the Museum of Ancient Egypt. What do you do first?

a) Draw a plan of the whole building, making careful note of any closets where a mummy can hide
b) Tidy yourself up after the long journey
c) Get to work interviewing everyone in the museum
d) Pay the museum snack shop a visit. You need to refuel!

☐

3

You need to check for important clues. What tool do you use to help you?

a) A Supernatural Detection Device
b) Your camera
c) Your trusty magnifying glass
d) Scooby-Doo's nose can sniff out anything!

☐

You uncover three trap doors. What do you do?

a) Carefully assess which one is safe before you open it
b) Pick one. Open it. Uh-oh, it's the wrong one! Help!
c) Report your discovery to the rest of the gang
d) Run away as fast as you can! There's bound to be something scary down there!

☐

The gang has split up to look for clues. You walk around a corner and suddenly spot a mummy ahead of you. Do you:

a) Set off in hot pursuit—this was all part of your plan
b) Look for the rest of the gang. You need some back up here!
c) Follow it, making note of any footprints or clues on the way
d) Sheesh, you're out of here! That spook is too close for comfort!

☐

6 It's time to head back to consult the rest of the gang when you feel a tap on your shoulder. Uh-oh! The mummy's right behind you, and he's not looking happy. What do you say?

a) "Ha! I'm not afraid of you!"
b) "Jeepers! You really should consider updating your wardrobe!"
c) "What a fascinating opportunity to get a good look at a supernatural being!"
d) "Like, excuse me, Mr. Mummy. I think you've got the wrong person!"

☐

7 The gang has put together a clever plan to try and capture that moaning old mummy. What part would you play in the plan?

a) I would be the chief organizer.
b) I would assist the chief organizer.
c) I would encourage the scaredy-cat members of the gang to take part by offering Scooby Snacks!
d) I would be the bait in the monster trap. Anything for a Scooby Snack!

☐

8 The trap has worked! The mummy is caught and unmasked as being the grumpy museum caretaker. How do you celebrate the gang's success?

a) That's great! Now it's time for the next adventure!
b) Tidy your hair, just in case the local paper wants a photo of the gang!
c) Take a tour of the museum. You've always wanted to find out about ancient Egypt!
d) How else can you celebrate than with an extra-large pizza with extra pineapple!

☐

How Did You Score?

MOSTLY As

You love being an ace detective! Just like Fred you enjoy taking the lead and getting really involved. However, you also know the importance of teamwork—it's the rest of the gang who make mystery-solving such fun!

MOSTLY Bs

You are stylish and smart and you love solving a good mystery—Daphne would be proud of you! You can be a little unlucky when it comes to falling into traps, but that's all part of the fun of being a supersleuth!

MOSTLY Cs

You are top of the class when it comes to detective know-how. You love nothing more than getting to the bottom of a mind-boggling mystery, and that takes nerves of steel! Velma would be impressed!

MOSTLY Ds

Just like Shaggy and Scooby you get spooked by the squeak of your own shoes! You've got what it takes to get involved in serious spook-busting—as long as there are treats along the way! The gang just wouldn't work without you!

Name that Ghoul

Can you match the words on the left to the words on the right to spell out the names of some spooky Scooby villains?

1 RED	BIE
2 CREE	PER
3 DRA	SY
4 GYP	CULA
5 ZOM	BEARD
6 GHOST	CLOWN

Scooby Snacking

Can you work out which two squares are needed to complete this Scooby scene?

Answers:
Name that Ghoul: 1. Redbeard; 2. Creeper; 3. Dracula; 4. Gypsy; 5. Zombie; 6. Ghost Clown.
Scooby Snacking: Squares B and D.

PAW PUZZLE
The Green Ghost is chasing poor Scooby, and he has left muddy pawprints everywhere! Count how many different-shaped pawprints you can see.
A
B
C
D
Me and my Shadow
Check out the shadows below and work out which one belongs to Fred.
1
2
3
4
Paw Puzzle: A-18; B-12; C-7; D-8.
Me and my Shadow: Shadow 2.
81

SCARY SPELL

Daphne has discovered this creepy cryptic code, and she can't understand what it says! Can you help? Take the first letter from the name of each object and spell out a hidden message.

Answer: The Black Knight is behind you!

THE UNUSUAL SUSPECTS

Help Velma crack this mystery! One of these crooks set all the rides at the fairground to autopilot! Crack the clues to work out which rogues have an alibi!

Write down your answer in the box below when you have cracked the clues!

CLUES

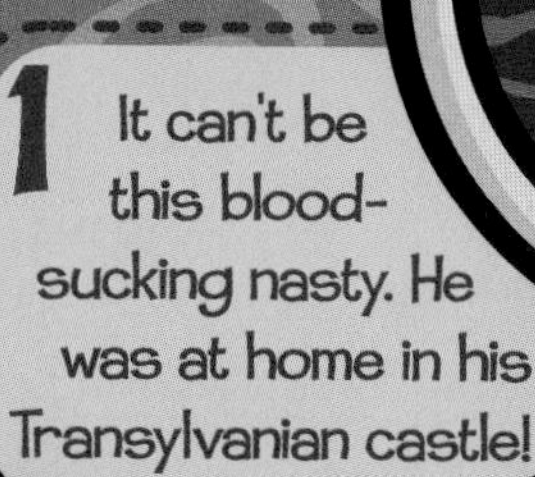

1 It can't be this blood-sucking nasty. He was at home in his Transylvanian castle!

2 Look! Something out of this world has left behind some footprints far away from the fairground. But who do they belong to?

3 Ah ha! A photo of Scoob skiing in another country. But look closer. Can you see which chilling ghoul is lurking in the background?

4 This crook was too busy burying his loot at a secret cove on Skull Island. He's left behind some important clues as to his identity though!

So you have eliminated all the crooks that were up to no good elsewhere. The crook that set all the rides at the fairground to autopilot is . . .

Answer: Funland Robot.

SPOOK SPOTTER
Mystery Inc. is investigating a freaky fairground! Can you help them spot all the spooks?

Answer on page 158.

PRIMO PUZZLERS

A witch has turned Mystery Inc. into frogs! Can you tell who's who so we can cure them?

Someone's given the Mystery Machine a respray! Can you spot the five changes to help the gang fix it?

The gang has found an ancient message on this stone tablet. Can you find what it says using Velma's decoder?

Ω3λλ δον3
ψου ηας3
χραχκ3δ
τη3 χοδ3

Enter decoded message here:

_ _ _ _ _ _ _ _ _ _ _ _ _ _ _
_ _ _ _ _ _ _ _ _ _ _ _ _ !

A	C	D	E	H	K	L	N	O	R	T	U	V	W	Y
α	χ	δ	3	η	κ	λ	ν	ο	ρ	τ	υ	ς	Ω	ψ

Answers:
Witch One's Witch: 1. Scooby; 2. Fred; 3. Shaggy; 4. Daphne; 5. Velma.
Mystery Makeover: 1. Stripe; 2. Bricks; 3. Flower; 4. Orange front; 5. Sign on side.
Code Cracker: Well done you have cracked the code!

Groovy Grid

Give Scooby-Doo and Shaggy a hand solving this giant word search!

C	O	O	L	S	V	I	L	L	E	M	S	C	O	L	V
Y	V	L	D	C	E	E	T	V	S	L	E	N	N	E	K
G	A	T	R	L	D	R	S	A	E	N	C	O	A	T	C
G	M	M	S	U	R	O	L	N	Z	O	M	B	I	E	O
A	P	F	O	E	C	P	O	D	A	P	H	N	E	O	O
H	I	R	B	N	A	T	W	I	T	C	H	F	R	E	D
S	R	S	M	F	S	Q	U	O	H	S	K	Y	R	A	Y
K	E	T	T	B	T	T	L	O	G	R	E	S	Z	H	B
N	B	S	M	U	L	E	E	D	N	V	D	Z	B	M	O
I	A	O	B	L	E	S	T	R	A	A	I	F	R	B	O
O	T	H	A	V	E	L	M	A	E	P	S	R	A	T	C
Z	W	G	M	K	E	Y	O	Y	R	E	T	S	Y	M	S

Scooby-Doo, Fred, Daphne, Bat, Key, Kennel, Snacks, Vampire, Monster, Van, Zoinks, Mystery, Clue, Shaggy, Ghosts, Velma, Pizza, Tombstone, Zombie, Castle, Ogre, Coolsville

Solve this riddle and then look for the answer in the grid!

I cook with a pot, and I cackle a lot,
I wear a hat, and I own a pet cat.

Answer on page 158.

Which Way Now?

Coolsville has been overrun by ghosts! Guide Fred and the Mystery Machine through the town without bumping into any monsters.

The tricky part is that Fred needs to stop and pick up each member of the gang on the way!

Answer on page 158.

Inside...
THE MYSTERY MACHINE
Ever wondered how the Mystery Machine works?
This top-secret fact file gives you the guided tour!
SPOOK TRACKER
This high-tech radar gives the gang
the location of any nearby monsters!
Binoculars
Shaggy &
Scoob's snack fridge
Daphne's sunglasses
selection
Emergency water supply
Daphne's
makeup bag

HOLO-MAP
Velma recently installed a holographic map system in the windshield, helping the team find their way anywhere in the world!
you are here
Velma's case book
EMERGENCY SCOOBY SNACKS
An emergency supply of Scooby Snacks to keep Scoob happy on long journeys (meaning more than five minutes!)
SCOOBY SNACKS
Grapple rope

OH MUMMY

Scooby-Doo and Shaggy are trapped in a tomb and can't work out the secret password to get out! Can you help?

CLUE: Cross out all the hidden words, then copy the leftover letters into the scroll below!

O	M	U	M	M	Y	P	E	N
B	O	O	B	Y	T	R	A	P
T	N	S	H	E	L	P	N	S
E	S	C	U	R	S	E	C	E
R	T	R	S	A	E	V	I	L
R	E	E	R	U	N	M	E	D
O	R	A	L	I	V	E	N	I
R	E	M	U	R	K	Y	T	E

MURKY
TERROR
MUMMY
MONSTER
BOOBY TRAP
ANCIENT
EVIL
CURSE
DIE
ALIVE
HELP
RUN
SCREAM

Enter leftover letters here to spell the password!

Answers on page 158.

FUN AT THE FAIR
Daphne and Velma have discovered some spooky shadows in the fairground. Can you work out what each shadow belongs to?
A
B
C
D
E
F
G
H
I
1
2
3
4
5
6
7
8
9
SCOOBY SNACKS
THE MYSTERY MACHINE
A B C D E F G H I
Answers: A7; B6; C3; D4; E8; F5; G2; H1; I9.

SPOT THE CLUES!
It's the Chinese New Year and Scooby-Doo and the gang visit Chinatown to join in the celebration. However, a mystery is about to unfold . . .
Soon after the parade starts, the Golden Mask mysteriously floats away. Then a spooky, cloaked figure, called the Hooded Ghoul, takes to the streets to do some haunting. With all of the frights and festivities going on, the gang decides to help Inspector Fong in unmasking this creepy crime.
Help the Mystery Gang to find all of these crazy characters:
Inspector Fong
Rick Shaw
The Golden Mask
The Hooded Ghoul
Tai Kwon Do
Scooby-Doo Kung-Foo
Answer on page 158.
HELP WANTED
CHINESE CHECKERS
MARSHALL'S ARTS
ALTERATION WHILE YOU WAIT!

CHOP CLASS
BUSTER CHOPS, INSTRUCTOR
KARATE
103
DOG DAYS
INN
LOW FAT
LOW FAT
NEXT SHOW
YEAR OF THE RABBIT
WAREHOUSE
BAIT SHOP
GONE FISHING
FISHERMAN'S WHARF
TITANIC

THE HAUNTED GRAVEYARD

Have you got the sleuthing skills needed to be a top detective? Find out with this super-spooky game!

Study the scene below for one minute. Then cover it up and answer the questions about it on the opposite page. The aim of the game is to remember as much as you can about the scene. So keep your eyes peeled!

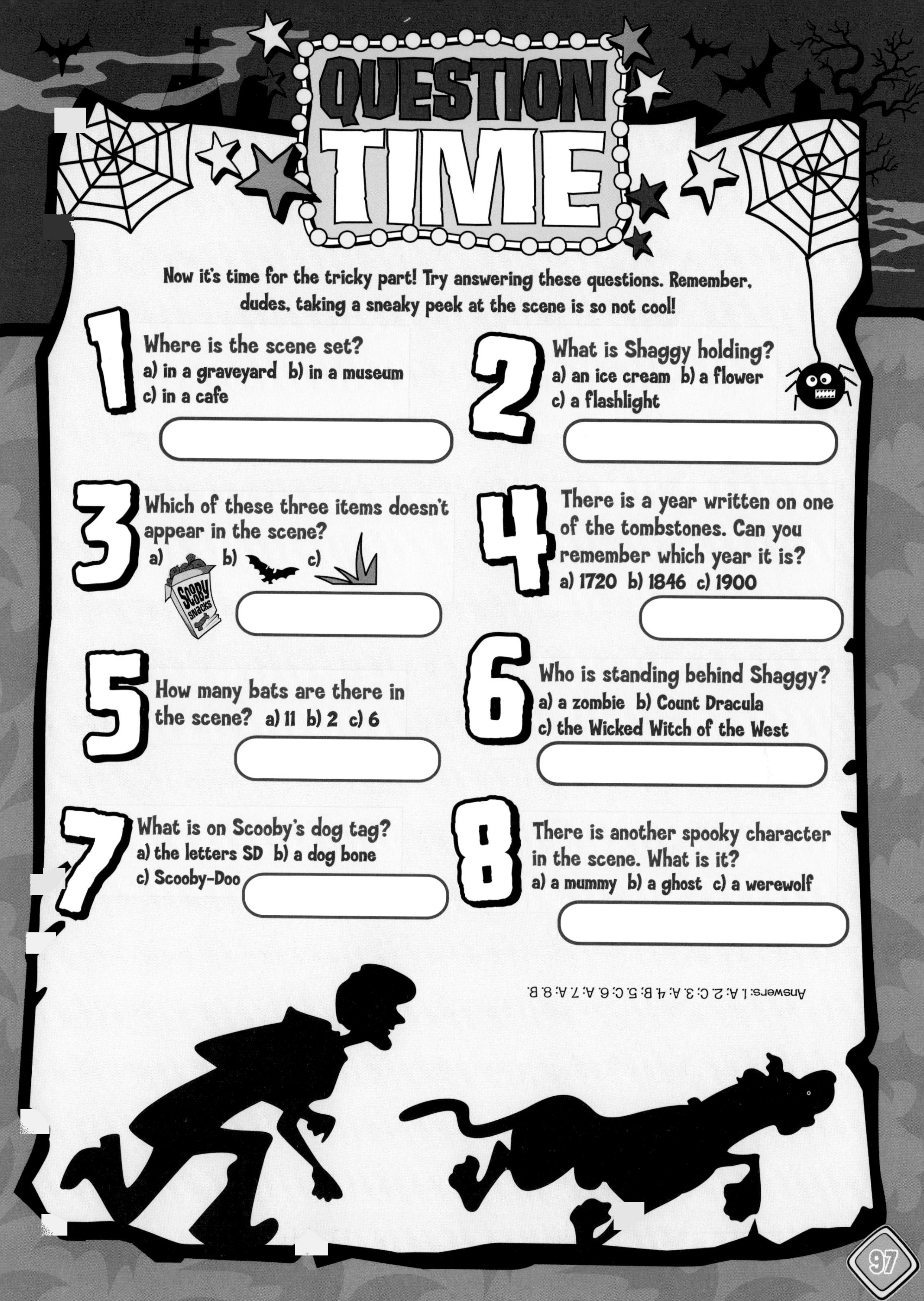
QUESTION TIME
Now it's time for the tricky part! Try answering these questions. Remember, dudes, taking a sneaky peek at the scene is so not cool!
1 Where is the scene set?
a) in a graveyard b) in a museum
c) in a cafe
2 What is Shaggy holding?
a) an ice cream b) a flower
c) a flashlight
3 Which of these three items doesn't appear in the scene?
a) b) c)
SCOOBY SNACKS
4 There is a year written on one of the tombstones. Can you remember which year it is?
a) 1720 b) 1846 c) 1900
5 How many bats are there in the scene? a) 11 b) 2 c) 6
6 Who is standing behind Shaggy?
a) a zombie b) Count Dracula
c) the Wicked Witch of the West
7 What is on Scooby's dog tag?
a) the letters SD b) a dog bone
c) Scooby-Doo
8 There is another spooky character in the scene. What is it?
a) a mummy b) a ghost c) a werewolf
Answers: 1 A; 2 C; 3 A; 4 B; 5 C; 6 A; 7 A; 8 B.
97

THE SPOOK SPOTTER FILES
PART THREE
Werewolves
1 2 3 4 5 6 7 8 9 10
Shaggy's Scare-o-meter
Like, the Scoobster and I steer clear of werewolves. When there is a full moon they transform into hairy, howling horrors. I'm totally wary of werewolves!
Villain Checklist:
Does the suspect have:
hairy hands
smelly breath
claws
fangs
VELMA'S VERDICT
Werewolves are tricky monsters to deal with. At the dead of night, they are scary monsters who attack anything in their path and, in the day, they return to normal. If you spot one, give us a call and we will help you to round up that bad guy.
R.I.P
R.I.P.
R.I.P.

IT'S BEHIND YOU
Grab your crayons and color in this Scooby-Doodle.

SCOOBY SCENE!
Keep your eyes peeled and see if you can spot all of the clues hidden in the scene.
The ghost of Rufus Raucous, a legendary magician, is causing chaos! Study the scene and see if you can spot all of the magical items hidden in the scene.
Answer on page 158.
NAILS
PRESS-ON

HAIR REMOVING CREAM
ANTI-BALDING CREAM
NOSE STRIPS
CAUTION MAGNETIC POLARITY
WHITENING GEL
WRINKLE CREAM
DEEP HEAT

MIND THE MUMMY
There are 12 differences between these two spooky scenes.
Use your detective skills to try and find them all.
BEWARE!
FREE FOOD!
Answers: 1. Shaggy's pants; 2. "FREE FOOD" sign; 3. Mummy hiding;
4. Flame; 5. Scooby's collar; 6. Eye color of the statue; 7. Sun; 8. Spider;
9. Tree; 10. Sand; 11. Back of mummy; 12. Scooby's shoulder.

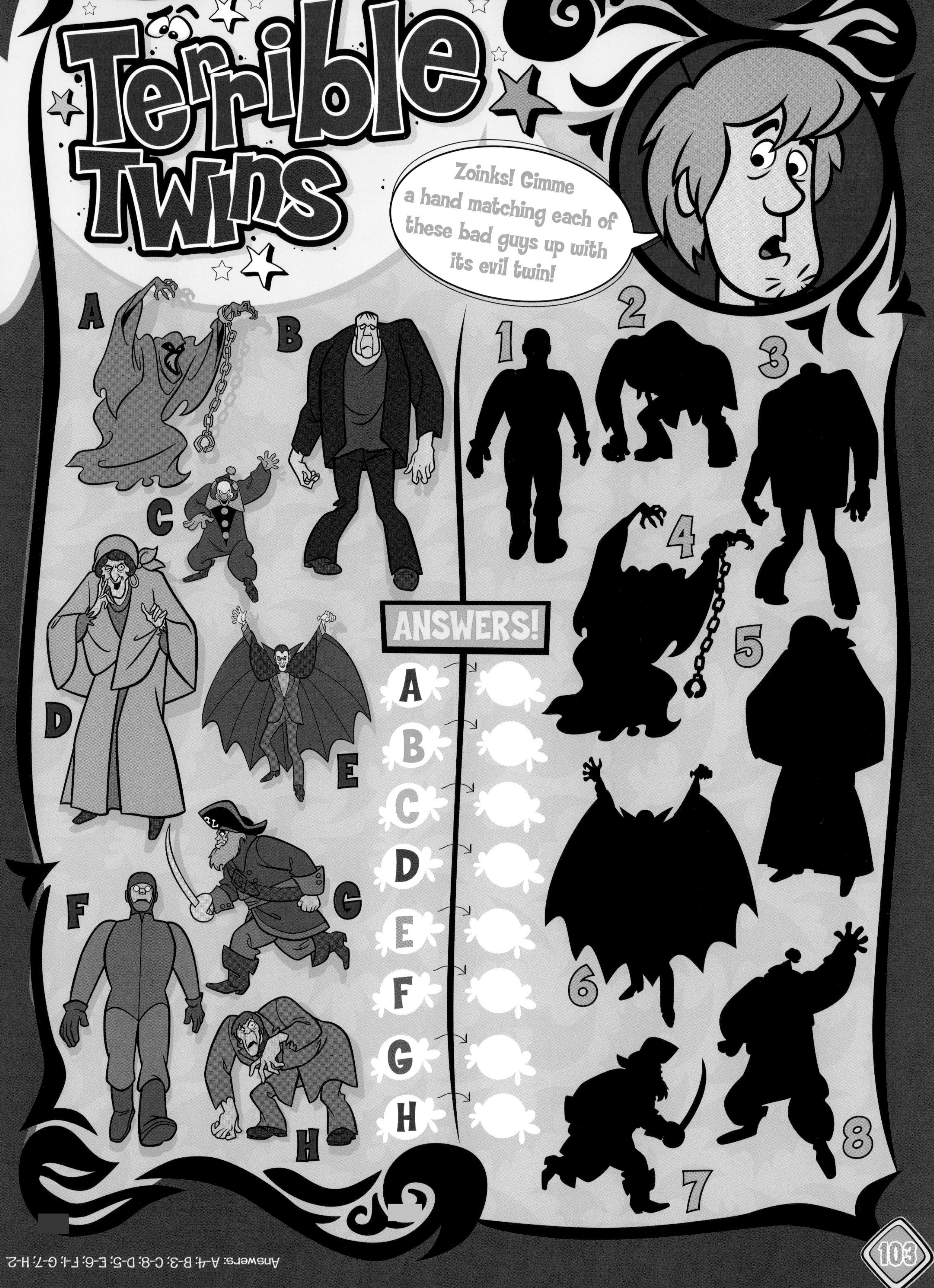
Terrible Twins
Zoinks! Gimme a hand matching each of these bad guys up with its evil twin!
A
B
C
D
E
F
G
H
1
2
3
4
5
6
7
8
ANSWERS!
A
B
C
D
E
F
G
H
Answers: A-4; B-3; C-8; D-5; E-6; F-1; G-7; H-2.

Clued Up
THE GRUESOME TWOSOME
The Creeper has got an identical twin but can you work out which one it is?
A
B
C
D
CRAZY CODE
Can you help Velma crack this code? She has worked out what some of the letters mean, but can you work out what the whole sentence says?
T W W F
U I F X F S F X P M G
T W
J T U I F K F X F M
T
U I J F G
104

Answer on page 159.

SCOOBY-DOO!™ WHERE ARE YOU?

Can you find all of the Scooby-Doo words hidden in the grid?

T	N	I	R	P	T	O	O	F	V
M	W	P	G	H	O	U	L	A	I
E	I	D	D	E	R	F	M	F	L
L	T	R	A	B	V	P	Q	H	L
L	C	T	M	P	I	L	O	M	A
I	H	Z	I	R	H	K	C	Y	I
V	F	Z	E	E	U	N	B	S	N
S	B	L	H	T	K	C	E	T	D
L	P	O	E	S	P	L	T	E	Q
O	T	U	I	N	X	O	W	R	K
O	L	T	S	O	H	G	U	Y	V
C	R	D	Q	M	P	I	Z	Z	A

DAPHNE
VAMPIRE
COOLSVILLE
GHOST
MYSTERY
PIZZA
VILLAIN
FREDDIE
WITCH
MONSTER
CLUE
GHOUL
FOOTPRINT
SNACK

There is one word missing from the grid. Can you figure out which one it is?

Answer on page 159.

SPOOKED

Even the Scooby-Doo crew gets scared of spooky things, y'know! Unscramble each word and then follow the paths to discover who is scared of what.

STOGSH

RDSPIES

WHCTSIE

VIRESPAM

TABS

Answers: Scooby-ghosts; Velma-witches; Fred-spiders; Shaggy-vampires; Daphne-bats.

Talk the Talk
Each member of the gang has his or her own special style of speaking! Use these top tips to learn how to talk just like the gang!
SCOOBY SPEAK!
1. The way to be a Scooby sound-a-like is to add an "R" to the beginning of everything. Say, "Raggy," instead of Shaggy, and "Ree-hee-hee!" instead of hee-hee-hee!
2. Scooby makes his words extra long, so "delicious" turns into "Reeeeeelicious!" and "help" becomes "Reeeeelp!"
REEEELP!
Like, this doesn't feel good, Scoob!
SHAGGY SAYS!
1. Like, obviously, you've gotta start everything with "Like!" or even "How do you like that?"
2. Dig the Shaggy groove! This dude loves to rhyme, so try saying stuff like, "hairy scary" or "groovy movie!"
SMART TALK!
1. Velma is a brainiac, so big, clever words are a must! Grab a dictionary and get wordy!
2. Start your sentences with, "Hmmmm," to show that you are really thinking about things.
HMMMMM!
THAT WRAPS UP THIS MYSTERY!
FEARLESS FRED!
1. Fred always sounds confident and brave. Try saying, "Hey, gang! Follow me!" to show that you are the leader.
2. Fred likes to have the last word: "That wraps up this mystery!" is his top phrase.
COOL CHAT!
1. When Daphne speaks, she sounds totally hip! Try saying, "Neat," "Groovy" and "Jeepers!"
2. Danger-prone Daphne often gets caught in scary situations, so screaming is essential! Shout, "Eeeeekk!" and "Aiiiieeee!" when you are really scared!
Oh look, a hair dryer and a compact mirror in one. Neat!

Grab a Snack
Poor Shaggy is super-starving!
Can you lead him through the maze and straight to the snacks? Be careful not to wake up Scooby-Doo on the way or he might eat them all first!
START
END
Answer on page 159.

MUMMY MAYHEM

Are you an ace detective who never misses a clue? Test your detective skills with this pyramid picture. Scooby-Doo and Shaggy are exploring a spooky pyramid, but they don't realize that there's a mad mummy on the loose! Study this creepy scene for one minute and then cover it up and answer the questions on the opposite page.

TAKE THE TEST

Now that you have studied the scene, cover it up and answer these questions. Remember, no peeking!

1. Where are Scooby and Shaggy standing?
   a) in a haunted house
   b) in a pyramid

2. There's a ghastly ghoul running down the stairs, but what kind of monster is it?

3. There is a large urn standing in front of Scooby. What is it decorated with?
   a) a snake b) a cat

4. True or false: Scooby-Doo is eating a slice of pizza.

5. There is a big urn sitting on the floor behind Shaggy, but what color is it?

6. Which of these objects doesn't appear in the scene?
   a) a chariot b) a box of Scooby Snacks
   c) an ancient statue sitting on a throne

7. True or false: Shaggy is wearing an Ancient Egyptian headdress in the scene.

8. What color are the walls of the room?

Answers: 1. B; 2. A mummy; 3. A; 4. False; 5. Dark red; 6. B; 7. False; 8. Yellow.

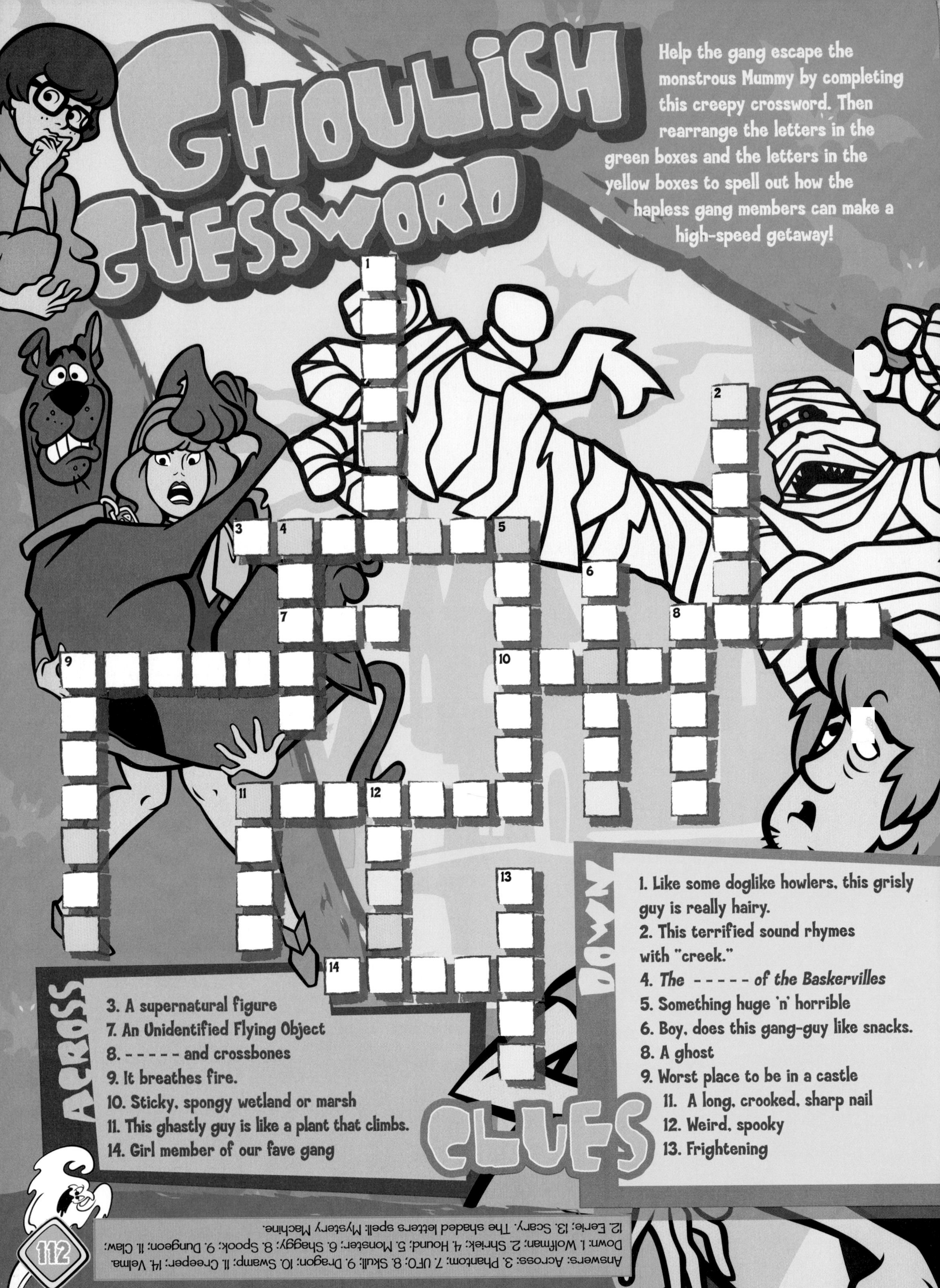

GHOULISH GUESSWORD
Help the gang escape the monstrous Mummy by completing this creepy crossword. Then rearrange the letters in the green boxes and the letters in the yellow boxes to spell out how the hapless gang members can make a high-speed getaway!
1
2
3
4
5
6
7
8
9
10
11
12
13
14
ACROSS
3. A supernatural figure
7. An Unidentified Flying Object
8. - - - - - and crossbones
9. It breathes fire.
10. Sticky, spongy wetland or marsh
11. This ghastly guy is like a plant that climbs.
14. Girl member of our fave gang
DOWN
1. Like some doglike howlers, this grisly guy is really hairy.
2. This terrified sound rhymes with "creek."
4. The - - - - - of the Baskervilles
5. Something huge 'n' horrible
6. Boy, does this gang-guy like snacks.
8. A ghost
9. Worst place to be in a castle
11. A long, crooked, sharp nail
12. Weird, spooky
13. Frightening
CLUES
Answers: Across: 3. Phantom; 7. UFO; 8. Skull; 9. Dragon; 10. Swamp; 11. Creeper; 14. Velma.
Down: 1. Wolfman; 2. Shriek; 4. Hound; 5. Monster; 6. Shaggy; 8. Spook; 9. Dungeon; 11. Claw;
12. Eerie; 13. Scary. The shaded letters spell: Mystery Machine.

WHAT'S YOUR SPOOKING STYLE?

Those pesky kids have taken on all kinds of creepy crooks, but what kind of spooky, kooky villain would you be? Take this quiz to find out!

1. All good villains need a spooky place to hide. Where would you choose?
a) a haunted house
b) a mysterious ghost ship
c) a spooky graveyard

2. What kind of disguise would you wear?
a) the classic ghost costume—you'd put a sheet over your head
b) you'd dress as a historical baddie who everyone is scared of
c) you'd dress as a scary creature, complete with fangs and glowing eyes!

3. What would your trademark spooky sound be?
a) a ghostly "whoo" and the sound of clanking chains
b) a chilling laugh
c) a haunting howl

4. Mystery Inc. is on your trail. How would you put them off?
a) scare Shaggy and Scooby with ghostly wails
b) jump on your ghost ship and mysteriously disappear
c) set a trap for Daphne to fall into

5. The gang have unmasked you as a fake ghoul. What do you do?
a) shout, "I would have gotten away with it if it weren't for you meddling kids!"
b) try to escape so that you can continue with your dastardly deeds
c) say sorry and promise never to be a fake spook again!

MOSTLY As THE GREEN GHOST

You would make a great Giggling Green Ghost! A bit of old-fashioned haunting is the best way to spook people, and that's what the Green Ghost does best. Like, Shaggy is totally terrified of you!

MOSTLY Bs REDBEARD THE PIRATE

Redbeard's spooking style is clever and tactical. He is a clever spook who hatches devious plans to get his own way. You would make a great first mate on Redbeard's ghost ship!

MOSTLY Cs WOLFMAN

The Wolfman thinks that you've got just the right approach to spooking! His terrifying appearance makes him a seriously scary villain to take on! Nobody's going to mess with those fangs, are they Scoob?

MYSTERY MAYHEM

Answers:
Knight-mare: Open sesame.
Over 'ear: A5; B3; C1; D4; E2.

Don't Be Snappy: 1. Scooby's tail; 2. Scooby's dog tag; 3. Scooby's eye has moved; 4. Scooby's spot is missing; 5. Crocodile's eye color; 6. One of the crocodile's teeth is bigger; 7. A water splash is missing; 8. Missing whiskers on Scooby.

Scooby-Doo!

GUESS WHO?

A werewolf has been terrorizing a town, and Mystery Inc. has been called in to solve the crime! Can you work out which suspect is behind the disguise?

Instructions:

There are six suspects. Look at the clues on the right hand page in order, crossing off ☒ the suspects that DIDN'T do it as you go.

WEREWOLF SUSPECT FILE #003

Clue 1
The guilty suspect does NOT wear sunglasses, so cross off anyone that's wearing any!
Clue 2
The guilty suspect is NOT wearing any jewelry.
Clue 3
The guilty suspect has lots of hair, so cross off anyone bald.
Clue 4
The villain IS wearing a hat, so cross off anyone that isn't!
Clue 5
The guilty suspect was wearing BLACK, so cross off anyone not wearing black!
Who is the WEREWOLF?
You should have crossed out five suspects and have only one left. Turn the page upside down to see if you're right!
Answer: F.

SPOOK SPOTTER

Scooby and Shaggy have run into more trouble in the jungle! Can you help them escape by spotting all the dangers?

THIS WAY OUT!

Answer on page 159.

Doggie Doodle

Follow these easy steps and create your own pictures of that super-scaredy Scooby-Doo!

1
2
3
Start by drawing a sausage shape for Scooby's neck and an oval for his nose. Add his collar, tag and ears. Add the detail to his mouth and nose and sketch in two arch shapes for his eyes. Finally, add the details like his whiskers and eyebrows.
Now it's your turn! Try adding your own Scooby sketch to the scene below.

ROLL UP, ROLL UP

Use your detective skills to spot all of the words hidden in the grid below.

S	T	U	N	O	C	O	C	M	B	A	F
G	H	O	S	T	T	R	A	I	N	P	E
I	S	E	T	B	G	C	O	R	I	P	R
S	T	H	O	T	D	O	G	R	O	N	R
S	E	D	I	R	G	R	Y	O	R	O	I
B	A	V	E	B	R	A	S	R	A	B	S
M	C	R	B	R	E	K	M	S	O	E	W
T	L	A	E	A	Z	E	E	E	R	K	H
Y	T	L	E	L	T	O	G	A	S	A	E
D	L	P	N	K	L	H	D	E	R	Y	E
N	R	O	A	C	A	R	O	U	S	E	L
A	T	O	C	S	W	L	D	C	R	A	A
C	I	H	S	I	F	D	L	O	G	V	V

HOT DOG
FERRIS WHEEL
GHOST TRAIN
CAROUSEL

GAMES
CANDY
SIDESHOW
MIRRORS

COCONUTS
GOLDFISH
RIDES
HOOPLA

There is one word which doesn't appear in the grid. Can you work out which one it is?

Answer on page 159.

SCOBY-DOO MINI MYSTERIES

Are you good enough to join Mystery Inc.? Find the clue or clues and solve the case!

The Case of the FREAKY PHANTOM

There had been strange goings-on at Morbid Manor, and Mystery Inc. was investigating.

"It was a guh-guh-ghost I tell you," Shaggy told the others once he'd gotten his breath back and recovered his strength with the help of several large snacks.

"Reah, a rig, rhosty rhost," agreed Scooby, nodding.

"Tell us what you saw," said Fred eagerly.

"I was, like, inspecting the refrigerator for important clues," said Shaggy. "Suddenly, Scooby tapped me on the shoulder. I turned around and, like, this glowing, green, freaky phantom had appeared as if from nowhere, and it started moving toward us, moaning. 'Zoinks!' I cried, 'Run!' We scampered from the kitchen as fast as we could, didn't we, Scoob?"

"Ruh Huh!"

"Then we ducked through a door and slammed it shut before racing down another hallway. The door handle turned, the door opened and the phantom followed us. If we hadn't managed to find a broom closet to, like, hide in, we'd have been, like, ghost toast."

"Reah, rhost toast!" said Scooby.

"I'm, like, still feeling slightly spooked," said Shaggy weakly. "Are there anymore snacks left?"

"Whatever it was that spooked you, Shaggy, it was no ghost," said Fred.

How does Fred know that it wasn't a ghost?
Can you find the clue?
Turn the page upside down to read the answer!

Answer: A real ghost wouldn't stop to open the door, it would just float straight though the door. Whatever Shaggy and Scooby-Doo saw could only have been someone in disguise.

Clued Up

It's time to get these spooky puzzles solved . . . that's if you're brave enough!

HAUNTED LIBRARY

Velma is trying to unravel the mystery of this spooky library! Each book has a matching pair apart from one. Can you work out which one it is?

1

2

3

4

5

6

7

8

9

10

11

12

13

14

15

Velma's Check List:

Write your matching pairs here . . .

16

17

THE MYSTERY BOOK IS NUMBER . . .

Answers: **Haunted Library:** 1 & 10; 2 & 15; 3 & 12; 4 & 6; 5 & 16; 7 & 17; 8 & 14; 9 & 11. Book 13 is the mystery book. **Picture Puzzle:** 1. Spider; 2. Werewolf; 3. Shaggy; 4. Witch; 5. Mummy; 6. Alien; 7. Bat; Hidden spook is Dracula. **Ghost Hunt:** There are eight ghosts.

Picture Puzzle

Identify each picture and write what it is in the grid. The number in parenthesis shows the number of letters in each word. The shaded boxes will reveal a hidden spook!

Ghost Hunt

Poor Scooby-Doo is caught up in a spooky situation! Can you count how many ghosts are haunting poor Scoob?

SPY GAMES
The gang are practicing their secret agent skills!
Can you help complete all the spy tests?
1. LASER MAZE
The gang needs to get to the end of the maze WITHOUT setting off the alarm!
Draw a line from start to finish WITHOUT hitting any lasers.
START
FINISH

2. CODE CRACKER

MYSTERY INC. SECRET AGENT I.D

SCOOBY-DOO

I.D NUMBER: 138149A

Well done on the maze! Now for a tougher test! Can you find the hidden word by crossing out every letter that appers TWICE?

B G D B R O

A P S Q H Z

C N C S Z L

L O R G E Q

Enter leftover letters here to spell the hidden word!

3. FREAK OR FAKE?

Nice work! Now the final test! Can you tell the difference between a real monster and a fake? Circle five differences!

Answers: Code Cracker: Daphne. Freak or Fake: Pants, tongue, eye patch, hair and tattoo.

MYSTERY MIRROR
DAPHNE IS CHECKING HER HAIR, BUT CAN YOU WORK OUT WHICH MIRROR SHOWS HER TRUE REFLECTION?
1
2
3
4
5
6
7
GET THE MESSAGE
The phantom is a phony and he has stolen a chest of treasure!
Fred has found a secret message, but he can't understand what it says. Hold the page up to a mirror to reveal its message!
Answer: Mirror 6 shows Daphne's reflection. Fred's secret message says, "The phantom is a phony and he has stolen a chest of treasure!"

PICTURE IT

Mystery Inc. is on the trail of a dastardly villain, and the gang needs your help! Use the grid references to copy each square into the grid below. Once you have copied all the squares, the grid will reveal a picture of the crook!

Once you have completed the picture, unscramble this word jumble to reveal the name of the Scooby villain! Write the name in the villain identity box below the grid.

HET OSGHT NWOCL

Answer: The Ghost Clown.

MYSTERY MAYHEM
SNACK STOP
Scooby-Doo is feeling peckish! Can you help him to find all the Scooby Snacks hidden in the picture?
CRAZY CODE
Use the decoder to work out what Shaggy is shouting!
DECODER
A B C D E F G H I J K L M
N O P Q R S T U V W X Y Z
130

Spook Search

Help Daphne find all the different kinds of spooks in the grid below. The words are hidden horizontally, vertically, backward and forward.

GHOST
APPARITION
MONSTER
POLTERGEIST
ZOMBIE
PHANTOM
MUMMY
SPIRIT
WITCH
SPOOK
GHOUL

P	L	Y	M	M	U	M	T	A	M
H	D	A	Z	K	N	O	S	X	P
A	H	R	Z	O	M	B	I	E	N
N	M	S	V	A	O	H	E	I	O
T	V	P	E	N	N	O	G	T	I
O	I	O	M	T	S	Z	R	A	T
M	C	O	Y	S	T	W	E	K	I
O	X	K	M	O	N	S	T	E	R
Z	H	W	D	H	R	K	L	T	A
L	U	O	H	G	X	S	O	K	P
F	E	D	T	I	R	I	P	S	P
W	I	T	C	H	J	B	Q	U	A

Answers on page 159.

SPOOK SPOTTER
Shaggy and Velma are in a creepy mummy's tomb! Can you help them escape by spotting all the spooks?

Answers on page 159.

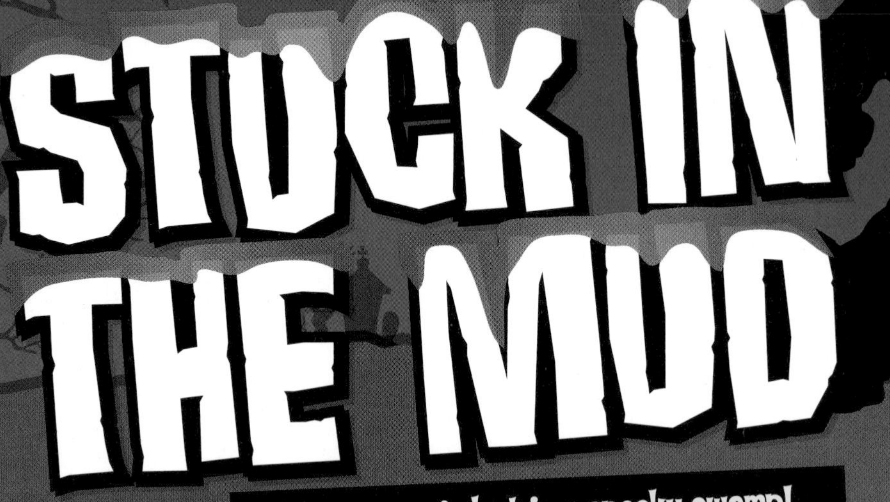

STUCK IN THE MUD

The gang is lost in a spooky swamp!
Can you help them escape by solving all the puzzles?

1. GRUBBY GANG

Fred, Velma, Shaggy and Daphne are covered in mud! Can you help Scooby work out who's who?

A

B

C

D

2. PUTRID PATH

Well done, you've worked out who's who! But now you've run into a REAL mud monster! Help the gang escape!

Start

Finish

3. WHICH WAY NOW?

Nice work! You've found two signs covered in mud, but only one points out of the swamp! Which one's which?

Check the correct sign! ✓

A

ONSTER'S
AIR THIS WAY!

B

T S WAY
TO S ETY!

Answers on page 160.

Clued Up
Monster Snack
Can you work out which snacks are missing from the picture on the right?
MESSAGE IN A BOTTLE
Shaggy has found a secret message. Can you help him crack the code?
A B C D E
F G H I J
K L M N O
P Q R S T
U V W X Y Z
???
136

Word Web

Can you fit the creepy creatures into the spider's web?

Ghosts
Alien
Hag
Spider
Robot
Tarantula

START! H

N

Hint: The last letter of each word becomes the first letter of the next word.

LOOK AGAIN

Fred can't get a signal on his Monster Sensor. Can you work out what he is looking at?

A

B

C

D

ON OFF

SCOOBY-DOO! MONSTER SENSOR

Answers:
Monster Snack: The slice of cake; the string of sausages; the carrot; the doughnut.
Message in a Bottle: The treasure is on Zombie Island.
Word Web: Hag; ghosts; spider; robot; tarantula; alien.
Look Again: a) a pumpkin; b) black cat; c) an owl; d) a spider.

WHAT'S YOUR FEAR FACTOR?

Are you brave enough to tackle a goony ghoul, or do your knees knock at the sight of a bat? Test your bravery with this crazy quiz!

1 You see some big, scary footprints on the ground in front of you. What do you do?

a) Investigate! Maybe there's a Bigfoot nearby!
b) Turn around and creep away
c) Nothing, you are frozen to the spot with fear! Help!

2 Fred suggests that you and the gang go to see a movie. What's your choice of film?

a) A comedy with a happy ending, guaranteed to be spook-free!
b) A really scary movie with ghosts and creepy sound effects
c) Something eerie is okay, but only if you've got popcorn to hide behind!

3 Mystery Inc. needs you to follow one of these creepy creatures! Which one would you take on?

a) An angry Zombie
b) A long-legged, hairy spider with red eyes
c) A very small bat

4 You're following The Creeper when suddenly you feel a big hand tapping you on the shoulder. What do you do?

a) Look for the nearest exit and get outta there!
b) Scream, tremble and say, "P-p-p-please, Mr. Creeper. Let me go!"
c) Grab the hand, perform your best Kung Fu move and tie that creep up!

5 Which of these best describes you?

a) Easily spooked
b) Brave and bold
c) Nerves of steel and totally fearless

HOW DID YOU DO?

Add the score from each answer and check your fear factor below!

	A	B	C
1.	10	5	3
2.	3	10	5
3.	10	5	3
4.	5	3	10
5.	3	5	10

FEELING THE FEAR! 3 — 20 POINTS

BOO! SHEESH, YOU REALLY DO HAVE A FEAR OF ALL THINGS SPOOKY! COME OUT FROM BEHIND THE SOFA, IT'S OKAY. GRAB YOURSELF A SCOOBY SNACK AND RELAX, SHAGGY KNOWS JUST HOW YOU FEEL!

FEARFUL! 21 — 35 POINTS

YOU'RE NOT AFRAID TO ADMIT THAT SOMETIMES YOU GET SPOOKED. THAT'S OKAY. MYSTERY INC. IS JUST THE SAME! YOU DON'T MIND FACING YOUR FEARS, EVEN IF IT IS AN ANGRY GLOOP MONSTER. AND THAT'S BRAVE ENOUGH FOR US!

FEARLESS! 36 — 50 POINTS

JEEPERS! YOU ARE JUST SO BRAVE! MONSTERS, BATS AND FIVE-EYED CREEPY THINGS ARE ALL IN A DAY'S WORK FOR YOU! FRED IS SERIOUSLY IMPRESSED. IT WOULD BE A BRAVE MONSTER TO TAKE YOU ON!

FUN FACT or Freaky Fiction?
Are these monster facts true or false?
1 Loch Ness, home to Nessie the lake monster, never freezes over—even when it's really cold!
2 Yetis are big, hairy monsters that live in woods in England.
3 COUNT DRACULA IS A FAMOUS VAMPIRE.
4 Shaggy is really scared of clowns.
5 A banshee is a type of goblin.
6 Bats only come out at night.
7 ZOMBIES ARE THREE-HEADED MONSTERS.
8 DAPHNE IS SCARED OF SPIDERS.
9 Vampires are scared of garlic.
10 One of the scariest monsters the gang has tackled was a Living Burger!
TRUE
FALSE
Answers: 1. True; 2. False, they live in the Himalayan mountains; 3. True; 4. True; 5. False, a banshee is a wailing ghost; 6. True; 7. False, they only have one head; 8. True; 9. True; 10. True.

GROOVY GAMES

Truly Amazing

Can you guide Shaggy through this maze to the feast of treats in the center? You need to collect as many snacks as you can on the way.

Answers:
Out for the Count: 3 owls, 5 bats, 4 spiders, 4 snakes, 7 creepy beetles.
The Great Outdoors!: Across: Backpack, Rope, Binoculars, Pillow, Tent; Down: Mallet, Marshmallows, Stove.
Truly Amazing!: There are 15 treats to pick up along the way. Don't forget to go back!

SPOOK SPOTTER

Mystery Inc. is stuck in a seriously spooky swamp! Can you help them escape safely by spotting all the spooks?

Answers on page 160.

RACE AGAINST CRIME

Mummies have stolen some treasure from a museum! Can you help the gang catch them before they escape?

1. DESERT DERBY

Can you help the gang drive the Mystery Machine through the desert maze? Watch out for holes!

Start

Finish

Well done, you got through the maze, but now you've got to cross a croc-infested swamp! Can you help?

Safely drive the van across by drawing a line from start to finish!

Finish

Phew, that was close! OK, you've reached the mummies' lair—now to get inside and grab the treasure back!

D W E I

H G K Z

Y E A P

O N T S

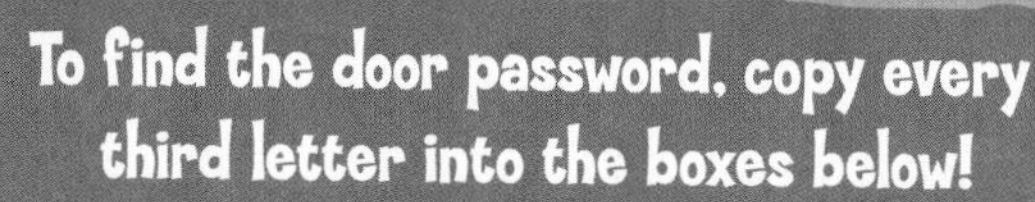

Answers on page 160.

SHADOW DANCE

MONSTER CROSSWORD

Jeepers. The gang is being chased by lots of mad monsters! Can you help them solve the clues and complete this creepy crossword before the giggling ghouls catch them?

CLUES ACROSS

3. A bony monster (8)
5. Another name for the Abominable Snowman (7)
7. The spookiest night of the year (9)
10. A hag who wears a pointed hat (5)
11. This insect spins webs (6)
13. Outer space creature (5)
14. Egyptian mummies live in them (8)
15. When a house has a ghost, the house is this (7)
16. A place where you find tombstones (9)

CLUES DOWN

1. A see-through, floating spook (5)
2. Half human, half wolf (8)
4. Another name for the living dead (6)
5. A female ghost who likes to wail and scream (7)
6. A nocturnal creature with wings (3)
8. The noise you make if you're scared (6)
9. The lake where a Scottish monster lives (4, 4)
12. He's a blood-sucking count (7)

When you have finished the crossword, the yellow boxes will spell out a hidden Scooby villain!

Answers: Across: 3. Skeleton; 5. Bigfoot; 7. Halloween; 10. Witch; 11. Spider; 13. Alien; 14. Pyramids; 15. Haunted; 16. Graveyard. Down: 1. Ghost; 2. Werewolf; 4. Zombie; 5. Banshee; 6. Bat; 8. Scream; 9. Loch Ness; 12. Dracula. The hidden villain is The Creeper.

Clued Up

GOONY GHOSTS

One of these giggling ghosts has stolen some precious treasure. Follow the clues to work out which one is the crook!

CREEPY CLUES

1) The crook is not a green ghost.
2) The crook is floating next to a red ghost.
3) The crook is not a red ghost.
4) The crook has two eyes and a mouth.
5) The crook is holding a clanking, ghostly chain.

ANSWER!

FACT OR FIB?

Can you work out which of Shaggy's statements are true?

1. Like, if I stand up straight, I'm more than 8 feet tall!
2. I carry a portable table set with a tablecloth, plates, food and utensils wherever I go.
3. I'm totally brave and love bumping into scary ghosts!
4. Like, I always wear a purple t-shirt and orange pants.
5. Zoinks! I really hate getting my hair cut!

ANSWERS

	TRUE/ FALSE
1	
2	
3	
4	
5	

PUMPKIN PERIL

Poor Daphne is trapped in a spooky pumpkin patch! Can you work out which path Fred needs to take to rescue her?

START!

FINISH!

SEEING SQUARES

Copy each square into the grid to reveal a Scooby villain.

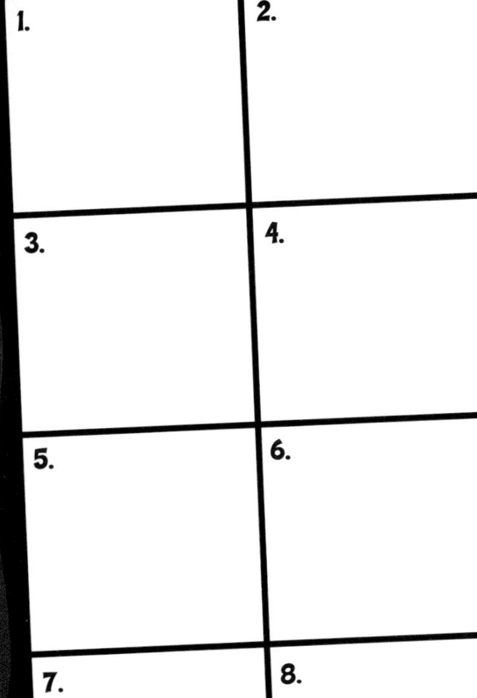

THE VILLAIN IS...

Answers on page 160.

GROOVY GAMES
WART
LOOPY LADDER
By changing one letter at a time, fit three words into the ladder to take you from WART to FILM.
FILM
Mystery Maze
Help Velma through the maze and collect all of the clues without crossing your path.
START
CLUE
FINISH
150

Answers on page 160.

SPOOK SPOTTER

The gang is being chased by a monster machine through a deadly desert! Can you help them spot all the spooks?

Check off as you find...
8
7
6
5
4
2
Bonus Items!
Five members of Mystery Inc.
Some Scooby Snacks
Velma's camera
Answers on page 160.

R.I.P

THE MYSTERY MACHINE
MYSTERY SOLVED!
Thanks for all your help!

Scooby Solutions

Pg 12-13. Spook Spotter

Pg 14. Escape from Mystery Mansion

Pg 18-19. Spook Spotter

Pg 22-23. Groovy Games

Heads Up: 1E, 2A, 3D, 4B, 5C.
Boo!: 1. Shaggy, 2. Scooby, 3. Velma, 4. Fred, 5. Daphne.
Desert Derby:

Pg 28-29. Wish You Were Here!

Pg 30-31. Spook Spotter

Pg 40-41. Wrap it Up

Secret Signs: The mummy has stolen the magic amulet.
Oh Mummy: Casket 7.

Pg 45. Scooby's Snack Attack

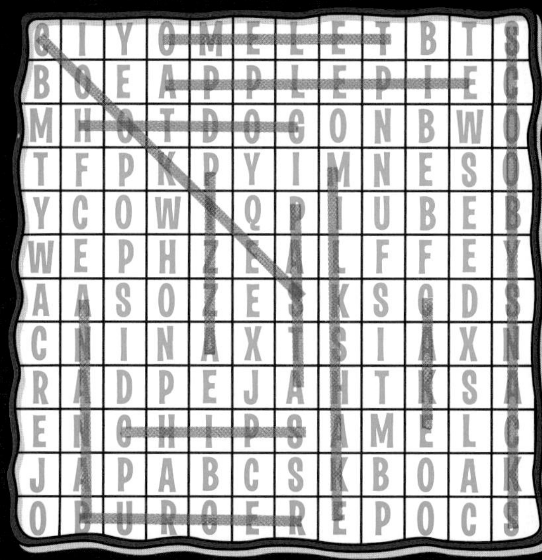

Pg 50-51. Spook Spotter

Pg 60-61. Mummy Mayhem

Pg 62. Scooby Search

Ths missing entry is Scooby Snacks.

Pg 66-67. Keep Your Eyes Peeled

Pg 74. Super Snackin'

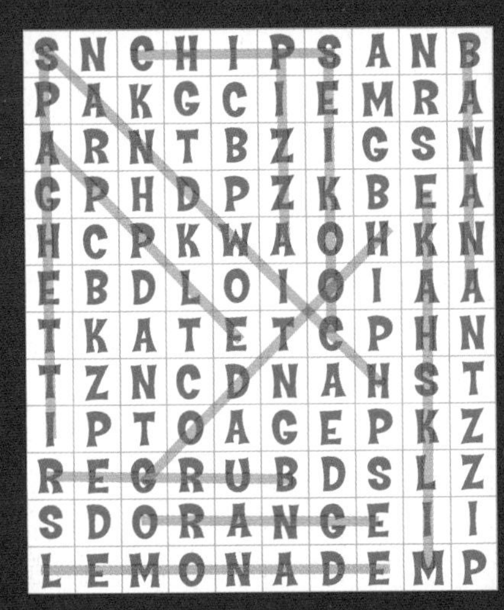

The missing snack is cake.

Pg 84-85. Spook Spotter

Pg 88. Groovy Grid

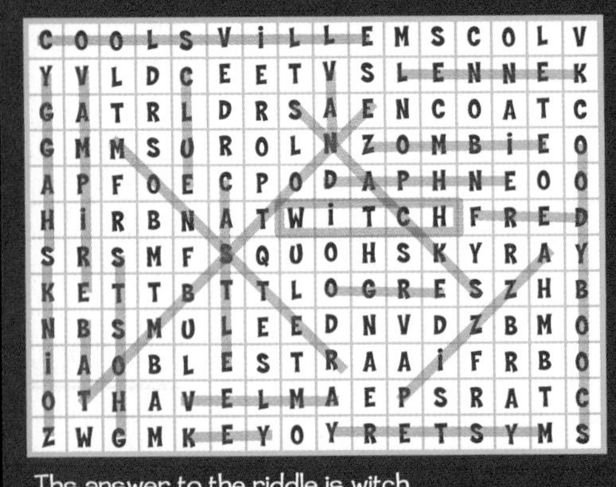

The answer to the riddle is witch.

Pg 89. Which Way Now?

Pg 92. Oh Mummy

The password is open sesame.

Pg 94-95. Spot the Clues

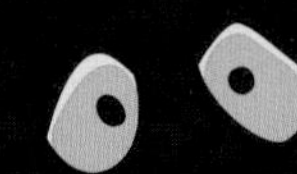

Pg 100-101. Scooby Scene